Charles Frederick Holder

All about Pasadena and its Vicinity

Its climate, missions, trails and cañons, fruits, flowers and game

Charles Frederick Holder

All about Pasadena and its Vicinity
its climate, missions, trails and cañons, fruits, flowers and game

ISBN/EAN: 9783337381622

Printed in Europe, USA, Canada, Australia, Japan

Cover: Foto ©Andreas Hilbeck / pixelio.de

More available books at **www.hansebooks.com**

ALL ABOUT

PASADENA

AND ITS VICINITY

ITS CLIMATE, MISSIONS, TRAILS AND CAÑONS,

FRUITS, FLOWERS AND GAME

BY

CHARLES FREDERICK HOLDER

AUTHOR OF "THE IVORY KING," "MARVELS OF ANIMAL LIFE," "A FROZEN
DRAGON," "ELEMENTS OF ZOÖLOGY," "A STRANGE COM-
PANY," "LIVING LIGHTS," ETC., ETC.

——— · ———

BOSTON 1889
LEE AND SHEPARD Publishers
10 MILK STREET NEXT " THE OLD SOUTH MEETING-HOUSE "
NEW YORK CHARLES T. DILLINGHAM
718 AND 720 BROADWAY

PREFACE.

The size of California is not generally appreciated. It is larger by ninety-three thousand square miles than all the New England States combined. In other words, it embraces one hundred and fifty-five thousand, nine hundred and eighty square miles of surface.

Los Angeles County, Southern California, is almost as large as the State of Massachusetts. It is a climatic paradox. Lying in the same latitude as North Carolina, it enjoys a winter in which roses bloom, and a summer cooler and more delightful than can be found in many eastern cities. Here the palm and apple, the pomegranate, banana, and every semi-tropical and temperate fruit, flower, or plant grow side by side.

The most attractive valley is the San Gabriel; and at its head, twenty-five miles from the Pacific, lies Pasadena — a city of fifteen thousand inhabitants, the home of a wealthy and cultivated community, the ideal health and fashionable resort.

The present volume is intended to give the tourist or general reader information regarding the conditions of life here, to indicate the points of greatest interest, and possibly make the strolls or rides of the reader more enjoyable by pointing out features, historical or natural, that would otherwise escape attention.

C. F. H.

Pasadena, Los Angeles Co., Southern California.
November, 1888.

TABLE OF CONTENTS.

LIST OF ILLUSTRATIONS.

PASADENA AND ITS VICINITY.

CHAPTER I.

SOME CURIOUS CONDITIONS.

Geographical position. The Japanese current. The peculiarities of situation.
Summer in winter time.

A S Pasadena is the best-equipped health and
pleasure resort, winter and summer, in this
country, bidding fair to compare in beauty with the
famed watering-places of the Rivièra, it has naturally
attracted the attention of people in every quarter of
the country; and every year hundreds of tourists
and others proposing to visit Southern California,
turn to the map and locate it near the thirty-fourth
parallel of latitude. They have been told that Pasadena is a winter summer-land, if the term can be used;
that flowers bloom the year round, and that Pasadena
snowflakes are orange petals. At first this seems
hardly possible, as, directly opposite, on the Atlantic
Coast, we find Wilmington, North Carolina,— a situation somewhat noted for cold and blustering winters;
at least, gardens are not kept up there from November
to March. There must be something, then, in the
surroundings of Pasadena that gives it singular and
extraordinary possibilities in the way of climate.

It is simply this: In the Pacific there is a large

current, known as the Japanese or Kurosiwo, that, resembling the Gulf Stream of the Atlantic, sweeps up from Japan around by Alaska, then, closely follow-ing the trend of the coast, is finally lost near the equa-torial Pacific. This mighty river of the ocean has an estimated width of five hundred miles, is extremely deep, and, most important, has a temperature that does not vary, from month to month, much from fifty-two degrees. The effect of this extraordinary current from the south upon what, in the natural order of events, would be a cold and forbidding coast, is to com-pletely modify it, to reverse things climatic; as if some of the strange customs of the Japanese, usually the reverse or antipodes of ours, were being carried out even in climate.

To fully appreciate the effect of this current upon the Pacific slope, one should start from a given point in the East during the dead of winter and follow the latitude to the Pacific Coast. On the Atlantic we leave intense cold; harbors are frozen, the farmer is housed for months, and the soil is to a depth of several feet frozen to granitic hardness. Following the thirty-fourth degree west from this, we shall find winter weather in New Mexico, and finally we sight from the grim yet interesting wastes of the Arizona or California deserts a ridge of lofty mountains. It is winter, then, in California, as the tops of the mighty Sierra Madre Range before us are capped with snow. We enter one of the narrow defiles, the Cajon Pass, and pass the gates of what over-enthusiastic Californians term Paradise. It is not paradise, but to the tourist who has left the snow and ice of the East it is, perhaps, as near it as can be expected. We have entered the great series of valleys, that fall from the Sierra Madres to the sea, and in a few hours are in Pasadena.

From Raymond Hill, East Pasadena, the site of the Raymond Hotel, we look down upon the city that has made such claims, and a glance shows its environ-ment to justify them.

Before us is spread away a scene from which Turner might have received inspiration, so rich is it in con-trasting effects, in marvelous tints, and in grandeur of conception. The remark is often heard that it re-sembles an ideal scene, and people who have traversed the globe state that its equal can seldom be found. There is no special object in view to call attention to, no surprises; it is the completeness of the picture as a whole, and the restful nature, that delights and im-presses one. The subject of this nature's study might be called " Winter and Summer," for this it is. The snows of winter are blowing here and there. We can see the flurries, and watch the white wraiths tossed aloft by the wind on the upper range ; yet, where we stand, the odor of the orange, rose, violet, and hundreds of flowers fills the air. We look upon winter from the midst of summer, and in a few hours can stand amid the snow-banks and look down upon this summer-land with its groves of orange, olive, and banana, and its acres of vineyard. The winter is upon the Sierra Madres that lie to the north of the San Gabriel Valley. The mountains range from two to eleven thousand feet in height ; opposite Pasadena they are from four to five thousand, and reach back for forty miles, constituting a labyrinth of cañons and ridges unequaled in any country under the sun. Fol-lowing the range with the eye, we see Old Baldy, a peak eleven thousand feet in height. It will repay one to ride down to Glendora and see the peak gleaming, with its silvery coat, through the green walls of the cañon that seem to form the frame for the picture. Farther along is Mt. San Bernadino, then San Jacinto, telling of Temecula and the Indians at Pachanga. Here the range trends to the south, forming Smith's Mountain, or Mt. Paloma, that overhangs Pala Mission. The Temecula Range, to the south, still parallel with the ocean, and down by Elsinore, takes us back, and we come to Mt. Santa Ana, with its altitude of nine thousand feet, snow-capped after every rain. From here a range of low mountains begins, that leads back to The Raymond, or six miles below it, under the name of the Puente Hills. We have traversed in a single glance many hundred square miles, yet the principal peaks are prominent features in the landscape without the aid of a glass. Turning to the west we see the Verdugo Mountains, blue in the distance; and, beyond them, reaching to the south, the Sierra Santa Monica range. A lofty jumble of hills rises directly to the west of the city, so we have, as regards environment, perfection; mountains appear on every hand, explaining the remarkable immunity Pasadena possesses from strong winds.

The San Gabriel Valley occupies the space bounded by the Arroyo Seco upon the west, the Sierra Madres on the north, and the Puente Hills upon the south. It is thirty-five or forty miles long, from east to west, and from the hills to the mountains about ten miles.

The climatic condition seems difficult to realize; but the story is simply told. When the blizzard blows in the East, the warm trade wind sighs through the **orange** blossoms here. When the ice is forming there, the birds are singing here. There is no lost time from one end of the year to the other. Nature seems always at her best, and the products of nearly every zone meet here. The banana and the pine, the palm and the apple, grow in the same dooryard, and when the summer comes, and sunstroke and other ills visit the East, perfect immunity is found here in cooler days and perfect nights. This is what is said of Pasadena, and these conditions constituted the magnet that drew hither the early settlers, and is still building up and populating this section of Southern California.

Fifteen years ago the San Gabriel Valley constituted several large ranches, owned by the Bandini family and several others, Spanish and American. Great live-oak trees covered large tracts, and the bare spots were overgrown with sage-brush and grease-wood, or carpeted with a variety of flowers found nowhere else in the world in greater beauty or profusion. The land was apparently valueless, except as a roaming ground for the sheep of the Mexican herders.

Los Angeles was a Mexican city partly Americanized, and the Spanish gallants rode out to the San Pasquale ranch, and about the old Mission of San Gabriel, to have their meets with hounds and horses. Then the wild-cat prowled about Raymond Hill, and the black-tailed deer found its way far down the Arroyo. In these days the San Gabriel was shut out from the world by the formidable range of the Sierra Madres, and the news was brought down or up the coast by sailing vessels or steamers, or, perchance, by horsemen, over the traveled roads between the missions at Los Angeles, Santa Barbara, San Luis Obispo, and so on to Monterey.

The Mexican war brought Los Angeles before the country, and the work of Fremont and Stockton secured it to the American people; but it was very many years later before a small party of men discovered Pasadena. They were Indianians, and, having been delegated by some friends at home to look over Southern California, with a view to establishing a colony, they entered the San Gabriel, driving out over the country from Los Angeles in teams. They examined the country well, went down into the lower counties, and finally returned to the spot they saw when they climbed up out of the Arroyo Seco, nine miles east of the City of the Angels. The peculiar position of the locality, its availability, its remarkable climate, absence from sudden change and all the features so disagreeable in the East, aroused their enthusiasm, and they reported that this was their choice. Such is, in brief, the early history of the place. People soon flocked here, the accounts being told by word of mouth, and in a few years Pasadena, the Crown of the Valley, as it was named, became a thriving village.

It had been learned from the Mission Fathers that the orange would grow here, and every settler had from ten to fifty acres laid out in orange groves. Experiment showed that here was a climate like that of Southern Italy, without the hot, debilitating summer, and that plants and fruits of every kind would thrive. So Pasadena became a vast orange grove — a veritable garden — attractive in summer, when the acres of vineyards were in bloom, and a place of incomparable beauty in winter, when the *mesas* were carpeted with flowers of every hue. Such a place could

not but grow; and, as settlers poured in, real estate
advanced, and the original holders grew rich, until
finally, four years ago, the railroad — the advance
guard of ripe civilization — reached the town.   At
almost one leap it became a city, and with rapid
strides has doubled and trebled its population, until
to-day it stands a city of fifteen thousand inhabitants,
with all the appliances of eastern cities of a century's
growth — a refined and cultivated community, without
a vestige of the rude elements that have formed an
integral part of the typical western towns.

The history of Pasadena would be incomplete without reference to the "boom."   The railroad made the
city easy of access, and simultaneously Walter Raymond, of Raymond excursion fame, began the erection
of a palatial hotel.   This afforded the first adequate
accommodations for a large number of visitors that the
city had had, and during the first six months of its season many thousand guests were entertained.

Among the visitors to Pasadena many were home
seekers ; and others, becoming enamored with the climate and country, also invested in land.   This, with
the speculative spirit always lying dormant, created a
real-estate craze similar to that seen in many towns of
the West during the past decade.

Property rose as high in the best localities as $800
per front foot, and for a year or more the city was
crowded with speculators, and almost every tract was
sold and re-sold many times.   Fortunes were made, and
enormous sums changed hands.   Conservative business
men, who had been through such excitement before,
prophesied disaster, and finally the people realized
that the time for speculation to cease had arrived ;

but, curiously enough, the terrible reaction anticipated
did not set in. Wild speculation had ceased, and a
gradual healthful growth took its place. Even Pasa-
denians were astonished, but the truth was that, while
they had been speculating in land, they had been planting trees, laying horse railroads, building banks, elegant business blocks, and mansions that would compare favorably with those in any city; so that when the
wild-cat speculation ended, and a shrinkage was looked
for, it did not come, for the simple reason that the
city improvements had kept apace with the highest
values given to inside property, and property in the
city proper was found to be worth all if not more than
was ever asked for it in the times of wildest excitement. So curious a condition of things could hardly
be found elsewhere; but the natural beauties and the
delightful climatic conditions of the place are its stock
in trade, and will always continue to exert their influ-
ence; and in the near future, when Pasadena shall
have become mature, when her palms, now fifteen feet
high, shall be thirty, there will be no fairer spot upon
the continent.

To-day we have in Pasadena a well-equipped, fashionable resort, winter and summer,— a city built rapidly, yet without a vestige of the rough element that is
to be found in the new cities of the inter-oceanic
region. This is due to the fact that Pasadena has
been built up by wealthy, refined, and cultivated people
from the great cities of the East; and, while without
maturity in years, she possesses all that time can bring,
especially as regards the social ties that bind and
mould communities.

PUBLIC LIBRARY, RAYMOND AVENUE.

WILSON GRAMMAR SCHOOL BUILDING, MARENGO AUENUE.

CHAPTER II.

The streets. Avenues. Public buildings. Points of interest. Car lines. Opera house.

THE name Pasadena is of Indian (Iroquois) origin, and means the Crown of the Valley, and is suggestive of the position of the city at the head or western portion of the famous San Gabriel Valley.

A deep cañon, the Arroyo Seco, richly wooded, a natural park, constitutes its western border, and its limits may be said to be the town of Ramona upon the south and the Sierra Madre Mountains on the north, a distance of nine miles, while it extends four or five miles in an easterly direction, its suburbs breaking up into the towns of Lamanda Park, Alhambra, and San Gabriel.

The city is laid out regularly in wide streets and avenues; the latter, as Raymond, Fair Oaks, and Marengo, extending north and south, leading to the foot of the mountains six miles from The Raymond. The streets and avenues are in many cases lined with cement sidewalks, over one hundred miles of this work having been already finished. On either side are attractive houses embowered in groves of the orange, lemon, and lime, or surrounded by a bewildering wealth of flowers. It can be truthfully said that nowhere can more attractive homes be found in so limited an area. It is the land of the afternoon ; people live out of doors, and have an inherent love of flowers. In almost every dooryard the rarest and most expensive eastern roses may be had for the asking. Houses are covered with the "gold of Ophir," and the " La France " is used as a hedge.

The city stands on a level tract, gradually ascending toward the foot-hills, so that the altitude can be very materially changed by a short walk. The Raymond Hotel, at East Pasadena, is one mile south of the post-office or the centre, and to the casual observer appears to be upon a level with it ; yet the business centre of the city is as high as the top of the hotel. Horse rail-roads intersect the city in every direction, taking one over the most interesting portions; and several dummy lines radiate, to the Devil's Gate, La Cañada Valley, and Altadena, the latter term being applied to the *mesa* or highland at the foot of the mountains where a magnificent view is had of the city from an altitude of about 1,800 feet. Here, overlooking the Pacific, some of the most sumptuous villas are found ; among them the residences of Dr. Green, J. B. Woodbury, and farther along the villas of Messrs. Hugus, Swartwout, Outhwaite, and finally Kinneloa, the home of Abbot Kinney, who, it is said, selected this spot as a home, after traversing almost the entire world in search of a climate suited to his requirements. Altadena receives another title from winter tourists, that of Poppy Land, as, after the first winter rain, acres of blaz-ing, golden-yellow poppies appear, transforming the upland slopes into a veritable "field of the cloth of gold."

Pasadena has three principal business streets: Colorado, extending east and west, and ultimately to reach the town of Monrovia, ten miles away; Raymond Avenue, extending from The Raymond Hotel directly through the heart of the city to the mountains; and Fair Oaks Avenue, parallel to it one block to the west.   These streets are provided with horse cars, and

ALONG THE ARROYO SECO.

built up with business blocks, which, in point of size, beauty, and general excellence, compare favorably with those of any city of like population in the East.   The streets are lighted by gas and electricity, and all the trades are represented.   On Raymond Avenue is the opera house, which cost $200,000, the most complete structure of the kind in Southern California.   On this thoroughfare is the Hotel Webster, the central depot, the post-office, and several large and expensive build-ings.   On Colorado Street are the banking interests, represented by three banks — the San Gabriel, the First National, and the Pasadena National Bank. Besides these there are many private banking firms. Here we find durable and richly designed blocks, among which may be mentioned the Fish Block, the Frost Building, the Arcade, and the Carlton Hotel Block.   At the junction of Colorado Street and Fair

Oaks Avenue is Williams Hall, for a long time the only theatre, and now used as a lecture hall. A natural history store displays all the curiosities of Southern California, from a gigantic tarantula to Chinese chop-sticks; and between Fair Oaks Avenue and Raymond, not far from the Hotel Raymond, we find a thriving "Chinatown."

Here the enticing game of Tan can be indulged in, the opium den on a small scale investigated, and Chinese heard as "she is spoke." Several stores contain the thousand and one objects attractive to the Chinese eye, as gods, historical figures, vases, plaques, sandal-wood fans, swords, banners, silk goods, fantastic jewelry, opium pipes, and finally, perchance, perched on the counter a genuine almond-eyed Chinese baby, not, however, for sale.

The public buildings of Pasadena speak well for its future. On Fair Oaks Avenue is the Young Men's Christian Association, a large and expensive building in course of erection. On Colorado Street near the extensive Carr estate the Union Club-House is rising, and returning to Raymond Avenue we find the Public Library building, the finest of the kind west of Denver. Here is a fine collection of books, and a reading-room containing all the papers and periodicals of the day. The reading-room is free to all visitors, and books are obtainable by paying a small monthly fee.

In the library are the rooms and museum of the Pasadena Academy of Sciences — which eventually will contain some of the finest collections in Southern California, among which may be mentioned the H. N. Rust collection of antiquities, ranging from the mound builders of the West to the California aborigines ; the

PRESBYTERIAN CHURCH.

Carr collection of fossils, representing the great and varied field covered by New York State; the zoölogical collections of Delos Arnold and C. F. Holder, while many other citizens of Pasadena propose to contribute their private collections, which will make the museum one of the most valuable in the State.

The principal residence streets of the city are Colorado, with the avenues radiating from it, and Orange Grove Avenue. The latter is the especial pride of the city, and with the Ridge, overlooking the valley, contains some of the most expensive and showy places. Orange Grove Avenue, which extends

ORANGE GROVE AVENUE.

parallel with the Arroyo Seco, or north and south, is about two miles in length, provided with cement side-walks its entire length, and planted with palms and pepper trees alternately. It is the fashionable drive, the Fifth Avenue of Pasadena.

A residence of particular interest is that of Ezra Carr, LL. D., a tract on the corner of Orange Grove Avenue and Colorado Street, reaching down as a vine and walnut grove into the heart of the city. Eleven years ago this was a barley field, and to-day it would pass for an estate half a century old. Dr. and Mrs. Carr are especially interested in botany, and their grounds contain choice plants and trees from almost every land under the sun. No better place could be selected to observe the possibilities of plants in South-

ern California. On the estate we find almost all the
conifers available in this country growing side by side
with the banana, pomegranate, guava, palm, and
papyrus. A running list of the plants of this place
alone would give, — grapes — forty or fifty varieties,
European and American — oranges, lemons, and
limes of all kinds, citron, apple, crab-apple, apricot,
barberries (hedge), cherry, currants, figs, guava, jujube,
loquat, pomegranates, prunes, plums, pears, peaches,
persimmons, mulberries, English walnuts, Preparturien walnuts, almonds, butternuts, beechnuts, chestnuts
(native and Italian), hickory nuts, pecan nuts, filberts.
These are represented by almost every variety known.
Among the trees we notice the cork, india-rubber, cedar
of Lebanon, deodar, annearias, yew, varieties of elm,
maples, hawthorn, eucalyptus, and acacias from Australia, also palms and pines of nearly all kinds. In twelve
years eucalyptus trees attain a height of a hundred
feet, and others in proportion. This estate contains
the finest collection of plants to be found in Southern
California.

The residences of Pasadena are rendered particularly attractive by the extraordinary variety of the
verdure. One can hardly expect to listen to the music
of the pine needles and look upon the ruddy pomegranate, loquat, or Abyssinian banana, or pick apples
with one hand and figs with the other; yet here this
and more is possible. The places are in most cases
surrounded by hedges, sometimes of the calla lily, more
often the Monterey cypress or lime, with gate-posts
of century plants that here often blossom when ten or
twelve years old instead of one hundred, rearing aloft
magnificent monuments of green and white.

The palm, grevillea, and pepper trees are most in vogue in street ornamentation. The pepper is a graceful fern-leafed tree, bearing rich clusters of bright red berries, and on Marengo Avenue, having been planted on either side, they form a perfect arch. On the drives of Bellevue and Waverly fine rows of growing palms are seen, which will ultimately attain a height of forty or fifty feet.

Pasadena has nearly, if not quite, one million dollars invested in churches and church property, and almost every denomination is represented; while lodges of various secret societies, military corps, and other associations are also found here.

The accommodations for visitors are particularly good. Large boarding-houses abound in various parts of the city, with graded prices; while several hotels, as the Painter, Carlton, Webster, Acme, and Crown Villa, are open the year round and are of especial convenience to business men.

Reference has been made to the horse railroad and dummy lines which cross the city. Assuming The Raymond to be the starting point, one can reach the centre by the Fair Oaks Avenue line.

From here the Colorado Street horse railway takes us down that fine avenue, one of the principal thoroughfares; one branch leads up Lake Avenue, taking passengers up the grade to Altadena, while another continues down Colorado, then turning to the right and ending at Marceline or Wilson's pasture, the natural park of Pasadena. Near here is the finest place, all things considered, in Pasadena, the country residence of J. De Barth Shorb, Esq. A line leads west along Colorado Street, crossing the Arroyo at Park Place, and skirting

the Arroyo on the west side to Linda Vista. Here are
the fine nurseries of the Park Place Company, James
Campbell, President, and B. O. Clark, Manager, where
a large collection of plants can be seen and many
choice tropical varieties, ranging from the beautiful fern
tree to the finest palms. Here also is the experimental
station, where all kinds of forest trees and rare plants
are to be reared and watched under the general direction of the forestry commissioners. A dummy line
skirts the hills of Linda Vista and takes the visitor up
the famous San Fernando Pass, or La Cañada Valley,
as it is now called. The view from here, looking down
the valley on clear days, is inexpressibly fine. Another
horse-car line leaves the centre, passing directly north
up New Fair Oaks Avenue to the Painter Hotel at
Monk Hill, when it becomes a dummy line and goes to
Devil's Gate, a narrow and beautiful defile in the
Arroyo Seco. Other lines are in progress of construc-
tion ; as the Monrovia line from Pasadena to Monrovia
and Los Angeles, a rapid transit road from Pasadena
to the City of the Angels, so that the city will soon be
completely traversed by rails. An interesting road
skirts The Raymond, passing the old adobe house in
the rear and taking the stroller away in the direction
of Stoneman's ranch, San Gabriel, andAlhambra. The
Altadena road, the Pacific terminus of the Salt Lake
road, begins near The Raymond and winds away up
through the poppies and orange groves of Altadena.

CHAPTER III.

An eastern hotel among the orange groves. Its situation. The view. Where the Raymond excursionists winter, etc.

IN Pasadena there are two eminences that are particularly noticeable : one is Washington Heights or Monk Hill, in North Pasadena, and the other Raymond Hill, in East Pasadena.

Upon the latter stands The Raymond, — the magnificent hotel built by Emmons Raymond and Walter Raymond, of Boston, for the convenience of the thousands brought to the Pacific Coast on the well-known Raymond excursions, and the general public. The Raymond and its promoters have done more for Pasadena than can be realized. It was the pioneer in Southern California of first-class hotels.

The Raymond stands on a hill just above the main line of the California Central, or Santa Fe, so that passengers from any State in the East are landed directly at its doors. In other words, you are taken from a snow storm in Boston, and a few days later find yourself in a Boston hotel, or with all the convenience and luxuries of one, amid the orange groves of the Pacific summer land.

For many years Mr. Raymond has been bringing large parties of tourists to Southern California, most of the time being spent at Monterey, Santa Monica, and other resorts, though Pasadena seemed to be the fa-

vorite spot. Curiously enough there were no accom·
modations here; hence it occurred to Mr. Raymond
that a large hotel where guests could have all the luxuries of the East, with semi-tropical surroundings, would
be appreciated. The present "Raymond" is the
development of this idea, and it has proved one of the
most successful hotels in the country.

The hotel stands about three hundred and fifty feet
above the surrounding valley and twelve hundred feet
above the Pacific, which is dimly visible twenty-five or
thirty miles away. To the north stretch away the
streets, avenues, and groves of the Crown of the Valley,
while to the south orange groves and vineyards succeed one another in endless profusion.

The writer has stood upon Raymond Hill in winter,
with travelers who have visited every available spot
worth seeing upon the globe, and the universal verdict
was that "This is the most perfect picture I have ever
seen." Turn which way you will, a view is had that in
its calm, restful beauty defies expression. Day by day
the scene grows upon one ; the mountains appear larger,
the changes of tint and shade more beautiful, until
finally the critic is obliged to confess that nowhere are
the snow-banks of winter and the flowers of summer
brought into such close and remarkable communion.

Looking to the east from the spacious verandas, we
see Old Baldy gleaming with snow; San Jacinto, white-
capped, ninety miles away, while the peaks of Santa
Ana and San Bernadino loom up like gigantic sentinels
guarding the approach to this summer land. To the
south stretches away Stoneman's ranch, with its old
vineyards and orange grove, the old homestead of
ex-Governor and General Stoneman, succeeded by

THE RAYMOND AND THE SAN GABRIEL VALLEY.

the San Gabriel vineyard, and the town of Ramona,
reaching up to the Puente Hills, among which in the
winter time rests a small laguna like a gem upon the
rich green of the slopes. To the west are the San
Rafael Hills, the hills of South Pasadena through
which we trace the deep arroyo that winds away to Los
Angeles, eight miles distant.

On calm clear days the blue waters of the Pacific
are distinctly visible from the veranda of 'the hotel,
and from the upper stories the white sands of Long
Beach, the vessels lying at anchor in the San Pedro
harbor from Australia and every part of the world, and
far out to sea, sixty miles or more distant, the peaks of
Santa Catalina and San Clemente.

The site of The Raymond embraces fifty-five acres;
under the guidance of an experienced landscape
gardener it is fast assuming a beautiful appearance,
and in a few years will be one of the most attractive
parks in Southern California. On the slopes are a bewildering variety of plants and flowers, and as we turn
and watch the snow-clouds and flurries, plainly visible
with the naked eye, borne aloft from Old Baldy, and
look again at the wealth of flowers in which we are
standing, it seems incomprehensible. Here are a
wonderful variety of trees: the cork, camphor, eucalyptus, apple, banana, palmas-fan, sago, date and
others, pomegranates, guavas, orange, lemon, and lime,
pines from Norfolk Island and from the borders of
the far north, all meeting here on neutral ground.

The hotel, which forms a landmark for many miles,
faces the south, and all of the rooms are sunny during
some portion of the day. Two large wings extend to
the north, and about the entire edifice are covered,
wide verandas, giving extended walks under shelter.

Everything is upon a large scale, — dining-rooms, parlor, ballroom, offices, and bedrooms, — and the general result is to give a light, airy, cheerful, and home-like appearance. Elevators and wide stair-ways communicate with the upper floors, and every possible modern improvement that would in any way tend to the comfort of guests has been introduced.

The building is lighted with gas and electric lights, and pure water is provided from artesian wells and the distant mountains.

Connected with the hotel is the most complete stable in the section ; the carriages having been made in the East for The Raymond service. A band of trained Shetland ponies and burros add to the ordinary features. The saddle horses are well selected and are familiar with the drives and trails of the vicinity.

The grounds are provided with all the appointments that modern hotel science could devise. On the west slope is a cacti grove where almost every species of this strange family can be seen by the lover of botany. Here are ornamental and drinking fountains, tennis courts, swings, children's play-ground, rustic houses, bowling-alleys, billiard halls for ladies and gentlemen, and many other features to amuse and interest guests.

A fine orchestra is attached to the hotel, and the balls and hops in the elegantly appointed ballroom make the season a round of gayety, while the hotel is so large that those desiring quiet can have complete seclusion.

The Raymond is at present open only during the winter season ; but the time will come in the near future, when the climatic conditions are better known, that its doors will be open also in summer, as the summers here

are far cooler than in almost any city in the East, and
one is guaranteed nights so cool that a blanket will
not be uncomfortable.   The hotel is under the manage-
ment of Mr. C. H. Merrill, so well known by his connec.
tion with the Crawford House (White Mountains, N. H.)
during the summer.

Mr. Merrill stands second to none in experience,
and to his good judgment and genial qualities much
of the success of this great hotel is due.   While The
Raymond appears to lie in the geographical centre
of the Crown of the Valley, its post-office address is
" East Pasadena."

Pasadena feels a justifiable pride in The Raymond
and its completeness as a hotel.   It is a feature of the
city, and a curiosity among hotels, and the crowning
monument of the great system of Raymond & Whit-
comb excursions, so well and favorably known in this
country, Mexico, and Europe.

Next to The Raymond in point of size is the Painter
Hotel on Washington Heights, and nearer the mountains, at their very base, the Sierra Madre Villa.   We
have, then, beginning with the Santa Monica hotels,
a chain, including Los Angeles, Garvanza, South Pasadena, The Raymond, the Painter, the Sierra Madre
Villa, and the proposed Wilson's Peak Hotel, that
gives the invalid every possible condition and altitude,
ranging from the sea-level to five or six thousand feet
above it, all within thirty miles.   Such conditions are
not found elsewhere in the habitable world.

CHAPTER IV.

SHORT DRIVES.

TO the lover of horseback riding Pasadena is a revelation, abounding as it does in an infinite variety of trails and drives all perfectly safe, and, in the main, accessible to carriages.

THE ARROYO SECO.

To the west of Pasadena extends the cañon of the Arroyo Seco, which means literally a dry river. In the summer this is the bed of a little stream which now and then disappears, really forming a good body of water, though out of sight, and in the winter after a rain bearing in its tortuous channel a rushing torrent of great power, the drainage of the great cañon of the Arroyo that extends a third of the way across the Sierra Madre range. At Pasadena the Arroyo forms a complete jungle, a most attractive resort for the walker or equestrian. Tall sycamore trees rear their graceful forms, while over the limbs and branches are festoons of the wild grape, clematis, and other vines, so luxuriant that they form a complete bower in many places. Live oaks, the willow, alder, and a variety of trees grow here, with vines and flowering plants innumerable, so that in the winter season the Arroyo becomes a literal garden. In and out among the trees

a trail has been worn, often leading down to the bed
of the brook; and here one can wander for hours at
Christmas time in this leafy retreat, with the birds
singing all about, and trout darting from the horse's
feet. Between the point known as Park Place and
that a mile or two south, the Arroyo is thickly wooded;
but to the north it branches out, becomes wider, and
low brush, cacti and the yucca are the principal forms
of vegetation. Here there is a good carriage road
reached from Park Place, which can be followed to
Devil's Gate, where, or near by, a road leads out of the
Arroyo. Equestrians can keep on and pass Devil's
Gate, fording the stream; but carriages take the road
referred to, finding another a little farther on, leading
down into the Arroyo again, where a cross road is
found. One to the left passes over into La Cañada
Valley, while that to the right carries you on up the
Arroyo into the mountains and to Switzer's. The
La Cañada drive may be continued for two or three
miles, then returning by Verdugo Cañon, a pleasant
valley, well wooded and attractive. A shorter ride,
and particularly pleasant for equestrians, is to follow
down the La Cañada road for a mile or so, then turn
to the left, and return to Pasadena through the hills.

By following the Arroyo road north we are brought
to the mouth of the cañon, hung with wild grape
and ivy; and for three miles, when the water is not
high, the ride, especially for those on horseback, is
a continual delight; the road winding between the high
walls of the cañon, skirted by rich vegetation and
abounding with flowers and ferns. A carriage can be
driven in as far as Bronk's, but the road is particularly adapted for horseback riding. The entrance of

the Arroyo at the mountains is about four miles from Pasadena proper.

LINDA VISTA.

Linda Vista lies three miles northwest of Pasadena, upon the west bank of the Arroyo Seco — a collection of houses shadowed by the San Rafael Hills that rise beyond. Here are the Park Place nursery and the Forestry Commission experimental station; but to the tourist the chief interest will perhaps centre in the trail that leads up over the hills just before we come to Linda Vista, by which the highest peak of the San Rafael range is reached, perhaps two thousand feet in height. The location of the trail is marked by a small house upon the ridge and a reservoir. There are two trails here, the one to the south being preferred. These are available for good saddle-horses, and from the summit one of the finest views down the valley is to be had. The climb can be made in less than an hour, though a longer time should be taken. On the summit a cairn is found, the " post-office " where people from all over the world have left their cards and names in poetry and prose.

A single glance from this prominence includes hundreds of square miles. Pasadena, with its wealth of homes, vineyards and groves, lies at our feet. The peaks of San Bernadino, Old Baldy, San Jacinto, and Santa Ana loom up beyond, while away to the east and south we see the towns of Puente, Monrovia, Whittier, Fulton Wells, and others. Turning to the west Los Angeles is below us, and far in the distance the blue Pacific and the gleaming sands of Long Beach, Wilmington, with the peaks of Santa Catalina, thirty miles off shore. To the northwest the range of Verango curves into line, with its fine cañons telling of game, while as far as the eye can see the main range of the Sierra Madres extends, breaking up into the hills and mountains of Ventura. All things considered, the view from here is the finest after that from the summit of the main range. In the descent we may see a coyote, wild-cat, or black-tailed deer, in the cañon, and curious owls look suspiciously at us from the bush below, showing that while barely above the city, here are all the elements that go to make up the secluded forest. The equestrian who does not fear riding through the bush will find many trails on these mountains, leading over the peaks; and a steep one, used at times by the writer, takes one down the western slope and out by Eagle-Rock Valley. It is, however, a good rule not to attempt to descend the mountain where there is no well-defined trail.

THE SAN RAFAEL RANCH.

One of the most attractive and diversified pieces of upland and lowland country in the near vicinity of Pasadena is the San Rafael ranch, owned by the Messrs. Johnson. It lies on the edge of the Arroyo directly west of the city, and formerly included most of the San Rafael range, and now is one of the largest ranches about Pasadena, embracing fine vineyards and grain land, and the famous Eagle Rock.

The ranch is reached from Garvanza (sweet pea)

through the tunnel road, and from Pasadena by the Arroyo road at the foot of California street; also by the Arroyo drive at the foot of Colorado court. The latter crosses the Arroyo by the Scoville bridge, and follows the winding trail to the summit, where a fine view of the city is to be had as well as of the surrounding country. A hundred yards to the left of the Scoville bridge is the county road, leading up a small cañon, but from disuse only safe for sure-footed horses or ponies. From the summit of the ridge, trails extend in every direction, leading out upon the spurs of the San Rafael Hills, affording the equestrian a variety of delightful rides.

Eagle Rock on this ranch is well worthy a visit, being the largest single rock in sight in the county. On its face a spread eagle has been carved by nature, having a particularly natural appearance at a little distance away, while the rock itself is a landmark for miles around.

The ranch was evidently once the site of a large Indian village, as near the residence of the Messrs. Johnson many quaint implements have been found: mortars, pestles, scrapers, and round stones probably used in some game.

SAN GABRIEL WINERY.

From Raymond Hill to the south, the country descends gradually in a level plain, ending in the ridge of the Puente Hills. In the immediate foreground is Stoneman's ranch, with its old vineyards and adobe houses, and about two miles away is a large conspicuous building, in the autumn surrounded by acres of green vineyards. This is Shorb's winery, the largest in the State. The vineyards, which stretch away a mass of gnarled roots to the eastern eye, are in the autumn a green mass of leaves hiding hundreds of tons of ripening grapes. The vineyard covers about fifteen hundred acres, producing the mission, zinfandel, matoras, burger, and other varieties of grapes.

This winery, the San Gabriel, is probably the largest in the world, the holding capacity of the cellar being about fifteen million gallons, the two crushing floors having a capacity of two hundred and fifty tons of grapes per day. If the stranger visitor visits this great establishment in the fall, the method of making wine can be observed, but in midwinter the machinery alone can be examined and the wines, dating back to about 1873, sampled.

BALDWIN'S RANCH.

Five miles east of Pasadena is the enormous ranch of E. J. Baldwin, or "Lucky Baldwin," as some call him. It is said that it was Mr. Baldwin's ambition to own from the mountains to the Pacific Ocean, and one would judge by an afternoon drive over the ranch that he had nearly succeeded. The ranch contains large groves of orange, lime and lemon, English walnut, and a large vineyard covering many hundreds of acres. Mr. Baldwin employs colored help largely, and their quarters and the store constitute a small settlement. The residence of the owner is surrounded in part by a lake, and the grounds are laid out in an attractive manner. An interesting feature of the Baldwin ranch is the stable, where many famous race horses have been reared and trained. Mr. Baldwin has a fine track, where the horses are exercised and educated for their trials in the East.

Here " Volante " was reared, " Molly McCarthy"
and " Lucky B "; the first-named being the best running horse among the five-year-olds in America. The
principal ranch of Mr. Baldwin is called Santa Anita,
and reaches up to the cañons of that name. It
embraces about 10,000 acres. Other ranches owned
by him in the vicinity are La Puente, 19,000 acres;
San Francisquilo ranch, 6,000 acres; Felipe Lugo
ranch, 3,000 acres; Portero Grande, 5,000 acres;
Merced, 3,000 acres, and Portero Chico, 100 acres;
46,100 acres in all.

ROSE'S WINERY.

Two miles west of Baldwin's, just south of Lamanda
Park, is the winery of Mr. Rose, State senator. It is
said that this ranks next to Shorb's as the largest in the
world. One may see three hundred tons of grapes
crushed daily here in the season. The wines are port,
angelica, sherry, hock, muscatel, cucamonga, claret,
blau elben and zinfandel. Large quantities of brandy
are also made, and the enormous casks and tuns will
well repay a visit. The orange grove on this ranch
comprises over twelve thousand trees, and here is also
a fine stable and racing track. The entire ranch has
recently been sold to a syndicate of English capitalists.
The oldest wine obtainable here is of the vintage of
1873. Some idea of the importance of this industry
may be formed when it is known that last year the
total value of wine and brandy made in Southern California was over $3,000,000. A million and a half
gallons of wine (a lake in itself) were shipped by sea,
and three and a half millions by rail. Many of the
large ranches are devoted to raisin-making, and at

present California ships about seven hundred thousand
pounds yearly.

The ridge extending from the Raymond Hill directly
east embraces some interesting ranches. The locality
was originally a fine live-oak grove, and still retains
much of its original beauty. Oak Knoll is the first of
the series, and includes a large vineyard and orange
grove and one of the most delightful drives leading away
down a small cañon and over a rustic bridge, taking the
rider pleasantly to the Old Mission and Alhambra.
From the crest of the hill the view is grand, comprising
the valley to the east and the country about Puente
and Duarte. Beyond Oak Knoll is a natural park,
dotted here and there with Mexican houses, and finally
the Shorb e'state, having the same view, and in its
grandeur of park surroundings calling to mind some of
the old English places. Near here is the Winston
ranch, with its ancient holdings, large groves and vineyards, all telling of an older occupancy than is seen
about Pasadena proper.

A ride on Marengo Avenue for two miles takes us
over a hill that rises abruptly just below Altadena,
known as Monk Hill and Washington Heights. The
monks did not originally live here ; the story is more
prosaic : it was merely owned once by a Mr. Monk,
who, had he held it until now, would have been a mil-
lionaire. Grouped about the hill are some attractive
homes, and upon the south slope stands the Painter
Hotel. From the summit a fine view spreads away in
every direction. In the near future this spot will probably be utilized by a large hotel, a purpose for which
it is admirably fitted. In the hollow near here you will
find fair rabbit shooting, and not far away hear the
love-notes of the pigeon, dove, and quail.

THE OSTRICH FARM.

A mile and a half from the centre, on the borders of the Arroyo Seco, between Devil's Gate and town, is the Pasadena ostrich farm, where it is proposed to establish a breeding station and carry on the business. A number of birds have been placed here, and as a new and growing industry the farm is well worthy a visit. Horses are, as a rule, terrified by the birds, and it is well for drivers to bear this in mind. The birds are valued at from $1,000 to $1,200 apiece, a high export duty being charged on both bird and eggs.

The big or full-grown birds are plucked about once in seven months, each wing producing twenty-five plumes, valued at from $3 to $5 apiece. Thus a first-class bird may net $320 per year, and if the bird is a female the value of the eggs would have to be added to this, a good breeder laying from fifty to seventy eggs a year.

The nest is a mere depression in the sand, generally containing twelve eggs, sometimes as many as sixteen. The birds divide the duties ; the hen sitting during the day and the cock at night. Forty-two days are required to complete the incubating process.

When first born the young chicks resemble the English hedgehog more than anything, being apparently covered with spines. After thirty days they are separated from the old birds.

The latter are given alfalfa; each bird eating about forty pounds daily, besides corn, doura, cabbages, turnips, broken shell, etc. A flock of ten birds will eat in a year ninety tons of food.

Hens in laying time lay every other day. Each egg tips the scales at about four pounds, and measures eighteen inches in circumference; so a good layer will lay three hundred and sixty pounds of eggs a year, or twenty birds, seven thousand two hundred pounds.

The chicks begin to pay at six months, when the first picking is begun. They live for eighty or one hundred years, and seem to have no special disease.

The possibilities of this business are great if conducted on business principles. In Africa it ranks next to the diamond trade. There are at least sixty thousand birds in captivity there, which produce $7,000,000 worth of feathers yearly, one half of which are sent to America, and upon which a high duty is paid. An interesting ostrich farm and zoölogical garden can be visited at Los Feliz ranch, on the Los Angeles River six miles from town. It is reached from Pasadena by Garvanza or by crossing the Scoville trail and taking the Eagle Rock Valley road, following it due west to the Glendale Hotel; the ranch is then in sight across the river.

CHAPTER V.

Millard, Eaton, Prieto, Las Flores, and other cañons. Las Cacitas. The Brown, Gidding and Wilson trails. Switzer's retreat.

TO the tourist the Sierra Madre Mountains are the most striking object about Pasadena. As a rule ranges rise heralded by foot-hills; but here the grim granite wall looms up as if shot from the surface by some mighty cataclysm, and presents from the valley of San Gabriel a singularly abrupt appearance. It might be readily imagined that this range or ridge of peaks constituted the entire system; but it is merely the beginning of a series of ranges that stretch forty, miles or more away toward the desert, forming one of the most remarkable series of cañons and impassable mazes in the country. It is a labyrinth that few have traversed — a mysterious region dangerous to enter without careful equipment, yet abounding in scenery of the grandest description. Deep cañons with precipitous walls, narrow valleys, huge trees, musical falls, places where the sun never reaches, weird caves, and mountain lakes are a few of the attractions found in this mountain system.

To the artist the changes of tint and color and the cloud effects present a wonderful field. Morning and evening there is a constant panorama of wondrous shades of red, pink, purple, and gray succeeding one another. This can be enjoyed or appreciated at a dis-

tance; but to fully realize the extent of the Sierra
Madres and their grandeur they must be ascended or
entered by some of the great cañon portals that face
the valley; and during the winter, when the greens are
particularly vivid, these retreats or green rivers offer
every inducement to the stroller.

ARROYO SECO CANON.

Facing Pasadena there are a number of cañons vary-
ing to some extent in their general attractions. They
are all about five miles from the centre of the city,
and can be followed from one to fifteen miles. The
largest is the Arroyo Seco, previously referred to. It
enters the mountains at the junction of the La Cañada
and San Gabriel Valleys, and next to the San Gabriel
is the finest and largest cañon in the valley.

It can be reached by carriage up Lincoln Avenue, or
in the Arroyo itself. You pass a wild-grape embowered
gateway, and are at once in the deep gorge of the
cañon. A fair carriage road winds around, crossing
the trout stream many times, and leading to Bronks,
three miles in. From here horses are necessary, and
the entire road is better adapted for the equestrian than
for carriages. It is an ideal drive, abounding in beautiful scenery and attractive situations, and in the winter it is often possible to gradually merge from the
summer-land of the lower cañon and enter the snow-
banks of the upper range. By following the Arroyo
Seco Cañon for fifteen miles, Switzer's camp is
reached, one of the most attractive resorts for the lover
of mountain life in the range, and to some extent calling to mind the Adirondacks without the black flies.

The Switzer trail is the result of months and almost
years of hard work by C. P. Switzer and his men. **Mr.**

Switzer and his partner were invalids, and, possessing an inherent love for the mountains, they determined to make a home here. As a result they have recovered health; and the place, having become famous as a resort, is visited by nearly every person who tarries in Southern California. An old Virginia welcome will be found at the camp, and an opportunity to try camp life under favorable circumstances. During the summer season, from March until the rains set in, is the most agreeable time to visit the camp. A burro train starts twice a week from the cañon entrance, making the trip between the hours of nine and five. A letter addressed to Commodore Perry Switzer, Pasadena, Cal., will place one in communication with the master of ceremonies.

From the camp there are many trips to be made, as Virginia Fall, with its beautiful cascade, the deep cañon below, where the walls rise and over-hang the chasm for two thousand feet. Here is the cave with its fantastic portière of moss, while the cool stream abounds in trout of goodly size.

A trail leads from the camp to the loftiest peak in the neighborhood—Mt. Disappointment, which has an altitude of about ten thousand feet, and from which a grand view of the mountain system is to be had. Beyond are the barley flats, where deer are often seen, and the tracks of bear and mountain lion not rare. The vegetation here is interesting, especially the yucca, which blooms in early summer, sending up a tall stalk sometimes twenty feet in height, from which springs a cream-white mass of flowers. The trail passes through fine groves of manzanita and many plants of interest to the botanist, while about the camp are large pines and other forest trees. The trip to Switzer's can be made by going up one day and returning the next; but several days should be spent here, and it is fast becoming a popular summer resort, and especially in favor of artists, who find inspiration and subjects in the place.

MILLARD CANON.

Millard and Negro Cañons enter the Arroyo at its mouth. The latter is small and accessible from Las Cacitas, affording a pleasant walk. Millard, on the contrary, is a large, well-wooded cañon, one of the most beautiful in the range. The approach winds up over the Giddings's ranch, then falls suddenly into the cañon, a road for carriages extending in for a mile or more. A good trail can now be followed, bringing the walker to the fall, half a mile away. The fall is sixty or seventy feet in height; of small capacity in the summer, but extremely picturesque : the water rushing from a hole in the rocks above, and gliding down a moss-covered precipice into the pool below, where for centuries it has aroused musical echoes. Indeed, the fall reminds one of the silver strings of some musical instrument. The water dashes into a stone basin, which has been worn out in ages past, until it forms an amphitheatre. Here the trail ends ; but the adventurous climber can, by using the roots that project to the right, climb to the higher bed of the stream, and ascend to the upper end of the cañon.

By climbing directly up the side of the cañon and keeping to the east, one may come out upon the Giddings's trail. Millard Cañon is one of the most delightful resorts in the range, particularly during the mid-winter season, when one may stand amid the huge green brakes, the delicate ferns, and wealth of foliage, and look up at the snow banks almost directly overhead. From Pasadena and back it gives one a horseback or carriage ride of about twelve miles. In time the trail will probably be continued, so that the fall can be passed on horseback.

Millard and Prieto or Negro Cañons form a triangular-shaped plateau that stands between the gorges. This is Las Cacitas, a famous health resort, the site of the Gleason Sanitarium. From it leads Brown's trail, so called for the sons of John Brown, Owen and Jason, who live here. This trail is one of the best in the range, and leads through a delightful region, abounding in many points of interest. It is the intention to continue the trail to the summit of Brown's Peak; at present it reaches two thirds of the way up, from which point a magnificent view of the valley is obtained.

On a conspicuous hill top the sons of John Brown have made their home, and many persons climb the hill to pay their respects to these old men who, many think, were, with their father, the first disturbers of the peace, that only came again when slavery was abolished. Owen Brown, the elder, a venerable appearing man, has passed through scenes that would have killed many stronger men ; and his famous retreat from Harper's Ferry is one of the most remarkable feats on record, showing indomitable energy and perseverance. Of the twenty-three persons who constituted the army of Brown at Harper's Ferry, only six escaped. Owen Brown conducted them over the mountains, swimming rivers, living on corn taken from the field, and of the entire party he alone lives to tell the story. Jason, the younger brother, was in many of the Kansas troubles, and escaped a violent death on many occasions by sim-

ple good fortune. Both still live up to the principles
that actuated their father, and are models of extreme
conscientiousness. Farther up the cañon or trail is the
picturesque log cabin and summer home of Henry
Thompson and wife, the latter the youngest daughter
of John Brown. Mr. Thompson was one of his staunch-
est supporters, and bears wounds received in the battle
of " Black Jack."

The Giddings' ranch, which occupies the plateau
over which the trail passes, is an interesting location.
Mr. Giddings is a nephew of the late Hon. Joshua R.
Giddings, so prominent as an anti-slavery leader. The
upper part of the plateau is the site of an old Indian
camp, so old that nothing is known about it. The
writer has wandered over it after the plow of the
owner, and seen many mortars and pestles of this ancient
people thrown up. From here begins the Giddings'
trail, available for horse, pony, or burro, winding away
up the mountains, and overlooking Millard Cañon for its
entire length. From here, also, a magnificent view of
the valley is to be had. Pasadena is at your feet, a
vast crazy quilt, or checker-board colored in many
tints and hues. An altitude of three thousand five
hundred feet or more can be attained here without
leaving the saddle.

To the east of Millard Cañon along the foot-hills the
largest olive orchard in the world has been planted, and
many small cañons cut the mountains, of interest to the
stroller. Then comes Las Flores Cañon, with its profusion of flowers, looking down on Poppy Land. A mile
or more to the east the great gorge of Eaton's Cañon is
seen, winding away much as the Arroyo, though it is
not accessible by horse. The walk in is over a trail

environed by bowlders torn from the upper range by winter torrents, and takes one into one of the wildest and most picturesque portions of the fronting range. The fall is within a short walk of the entrance, and represents the drainage of a large area.

These cañons are comparatively dry in summer, yet the stream in winter is often a rushing torrent, carrying all before it. The writer was once detained for two days by the Millard Cañon stream, that in midsummer almost disappears. A cloud-burst in the mountain filled it to overflowing, and the noise of the bowlders, literally bowled down from the upper range, was deafening and a continuous reverberating roar. Such occurrences are rare, and usually the cañons, winter and summer, are delightful retreats — rivers of green, in which one may stand and look upward and see the blue sky outlined far above.

East of Eaton Cañon are some of the finest of the upland ranches: Kinneloa, reaching far up to the mountains, embracing many acres of oranges of every variety from the mandarin to the Washington Navel. The residence of the owner is one embowered, winter and summer, with flowers and tropical plants, vines, and trees. Below is Edge Cliff, the home of Dr. Murry; and near by is the Sanitarium; while the Sierra Madre Villa, the residence of Mr. Carter, and many others lead one to the towns of Sierra Madre, Monrovia, and beyond. At Sierra Madre we find a delightful location. Here is the home of Professor Lewis, R. A., whose studio is the centre of art interest here, and whose sketches and studies of the mountains have attracted attention in Europe.

VERDUGO CANONS.

The range of hills known as the Verdugo Mountains, seen outlined in blue from Pasadena over the San Rafael hills, abounds in pleasant cañons, from nearly all of which trails lead up to the summits. The author has made the ascent on horseback, and it is practicable to those who do not mind some hard riding in the brush. Once on the peaks, they can be followed for a long distance, affording views of the country, particularly to the west, that well repay the climb — Los Angeles is at your feet, and the valley before us stretches away as far as the eye can reach toward Ventura. The town of Glendale is marked by the large hotel, and the patch of live-oaks nestled beneath the foot-hills of the Sierra Santa Monica range, or its western terminus across the Los Angeles River, tell of the ostrich farm and Beauchamp's Zoölogical Garden.

The Verdugo (Green) Mountains are eight miles from Pasadena, and can be reached by the La Cañada Valley road, the drive down the big Verdugo Cañon being particularly pleasant, or by crossing Scoville's trail and taking the Eagle Rock Valley road, or by Garvanza. Old Mexican houses, camps of semi-Indians, and quaint hovels here and there lend an interest to the trip. To the equestrian a cross-country cut, taking the hills as they come, is often productive of much pleasure, not to speak of torn habits. The Verdugo Hills afford fair deer shooting in season. A good pack of fox hounds and some one familiar with the range, as Mr. Jean Giddings, are indispensable to the sport.

LINCOLN PARK.

We are in imagination following the mountain ranges around to the west, and, returning from the Verdugo Hills, pass Garvanza. Directly opposite and extending along the arroyo edge are a series of hills, small cañons, and ravines, forming delightful rides and walks. The hills overlook the cities of Pasadena and Los Angeles, and are rich in green in the winter ; while the perennial live-oaks that skirt their borders give them an attractive appearance even in summer. In the miniature valleys the wild mustard grows, rising five or six feet in slender shafts, topped with yellow blossoms, as if a shower of floss had fallen from the skies. From the hill top this is a veritable golden-yellow sea, shimmering and gleaming in the cool trade wind. Then descend and ride in the golden mass, the flowers meeting around your horse's head, see the bunches of violets springing up at every step, watch the meadow-lark rise, and hear its glorious melody, — all this, on Christmas day, perhaps, is the privilege of the winter stroller in the San Gabriel. Under the oaks and the vine-clad sycamores of the adjacent arroyo the Pasadena Hunt Club has its meets, and follows the hounds after the wild cat and coyote, that abound here.

PUENTE HILLS.

To the east of the Lincoln Park hills, that shadow the little town of that name and reach away quite to Los Angeles, and through which winds the old adobe road to the City of the Angels, is a ridge of low hills that trend to the east, seemingly culminating in Mount Santa Ana, in the southern country, where Modjeska has taken up her summer home in the San Antonio Cañon. In

the winter they are rich in greens, and one can ride
over them on horseback to much profit. Several
passes or cuts bear roads leading to the south, Santa
Ana, Orange, and San Juan Capistrano. The range
is about three miles directly south of The Raymond,
and among the hills in winter is a small lake that in
season abounds in duck and geese. The hills to the
east are cut by the San Gabriel River, and on the south
slope is the town of Whittier, with Santa Fè Springs
three miles away. The river bottom, with its wealth of
trees, and the vicinity is of particular interest to tourists
on account of the many old Mexican ranches. Old
adobe houses and ruins are met with here and there,
and men, women, and children, to whom the English
language is an unknown tongue. The old Spanish
customs still prevail. Huge grape vines form a *ramada*,
or out-door room ; the stone *metate*, mortar and pestle,
are familiar objects in the hard, smooth dooryard,
while red peppers and an odor of tomalies give a dis-
tinctively foreign flavor to the scene.

The writer has enjoyed many of these localities when
riding over the country on horseback. In this manner
out-of-the-way places, houses, and bits of quaint Spanish
or Mexican life, unsuspected so near the great and growing American cities, can be visited. They are all within
a day's drive from Pasadena. If in winter after a rain,
the panorama of the range capped with snow, seen over
green orange trees, is incomparable, indeed, inspiring ;
while in summer the succession of tints on the slopes,
the deepening of the shadows as they creep from the
cañons, and the fading of the glow, finally changing
from purple to deeper gloom, are spectacles peculiar to
the southern range.

CHAPTER VI.

THE SAN GABRIEL MISSION.

Its history. The early fathers and Indians. San Gabriel. El Molino. Old
people. The work of the fathers. Famous gardens. Old vines and palms.

PASADENA proper is the prototype of an eastern
city, with a pedigree dating back into the last century. Its residences show the marks of eastern culture
and refinement ; and, if the stranger could be suddenly
set down on Orange Grove Avenue or Colorado Street,
he or she might well imagine themselves in some New
England city of beautiful homes, where, in some mysterious manner, palms, bananas, guavas, and pomegranates were growing.

In other words, though built up in a country where
the traditions are all of Spanish or Mexican origin,
Pasadena is a thoroughly American city, and its Mexican inhabitants can be almost counted on the fingers.
This is somewhat disappointing to the tourist who
would prefer to find some relics of an older occupation,
a Sonora town, perchance. If Pasadena does not possess this feature in her immediate borders, she has in
San Gabriel, an adjoining town, really a suburb three
miles away, one of the most interesting Spanish settlements in Southern California. From The Raymond, in
East Pasadena, San Gabriel is reached by riding southeast by Stoneman's ranch; and from Pasadena proper a
delightful way is by Oak Knoll. San Gabriel is, according to some jovial authorities, the original spot where
a man was killed to start a graveyard. People rarely

die here, so we are told; at least, they seem disposed
to live on to preposterous ages. The author enjoyed
the acquaintance of an old lady of San Gabriel who, it
was said, was at least one hundred and seventeen years
old. The last time I visited her, some weeks before
her death, she sat with her grandchild, herself an old
woman, upon a rude bed against the wall, in which were
cracks through which the wind blew freely. Perhaps
it was this very life in the open air that produced this
longevity. Another old lady, Señora Eulalia Perez de
Guilen, died here in 1878, at the ripe old age of one
hundred and forty years. She was born below San
Diego, in Lower California, in 1735, three years
after the birth of George Washington; in 1854 she mar-
ried Francisco Villabobas de Zavia, who died aged one
hundred and twelve years. Many old people still
reside here.

San Gabriel village abounds in old places and
ranches. The main street is truly Mexican, and
given over to wine shops. Low crumbling adobes are
sandwiched in between John's laundry; and black-
haired children, men with broad sombreros, on horses
accoutred after the Mexican fashion, the saddles gaudily
bedecked with silver, clanking spurs, all point to the
conclusion that here, indeed, is a Mexican town. On
Sundays, when the wine shops are thronged, the musical
notes of the old Mission bells — the same that have
called the faithful for many years — come stealing over
the senses like a memory of the past. Everything
about the town but the wine is old. The adobes
are the same that were in use nearly a hundred years
ago; and lofty palms, grape vines like trees, old *ram-
adas*, point to an ancient occupation. The town has

the appearance of going to decay, and in this instance appearances are not deceitful. In former days this locality was the great agricultural centre of Southern California, and around the old Mission was grouped a municipality so powerful that this very fact produced its downfall by exciting the jealousy of the powers that were.

The most important and noticeable remnant of this olden time is the San Gabriel Mission, a long adobe building at the end of the principal street of the town.

THE SAN GABRIEL MISSION.

On Sundays and feast days it is open for service, and at any time tourists may visit it, though expected to give the person who shows them about some little contribution for the church or poor. This is not demanded or even asked, the Mexicans being proverbially modest and retiring. The old building has lately been repaired, and presents a good appearance, though its interior decorations may verge on the barbaric.

On entering from the warm outside air, the chill is sensibly felt, and it seems damp, though not, in fact. The walls are plastered in a rough manner, and ornamented with rude paintings representing the saints and other subjects dear to the Church of Rome. At the west end stands the altar, with its meagre decorations, and about the asphaltum floor are a few benches, the worshipers formerly sitting upon the floor. On the east end is a gallery, reached from without by stone steps, and here a choir of Mexican women sing. A chime of four bells hangs in the tower, and much controversy has risen as to where they were cast. According to the old tradition of the Mission, they were sent from Spain; but, according to Father Bot, there is an entirely different version and probably the true one.

This authority states that the largest bell was bought from a North Prussia ship, that anchored at San Pedro, and paid for in the coin of the realm—hides, tallow, etc. Another bell was cast in Boston, and paid for in the same way; and the rest may have been cast in Spain. The tower is cut for six bells, and a mock bell of wood filled one of the spaces for some time; this and another bell have mysteriously disappeared, and perhaps ornament the collection of some relic hunter. With its high windows (so that bullets could not enter), its heavy, thick walls, and quaint furniture, the old Mission is one of the most interesting features of the locality.

On the west end of the Mission building is the house of the presiding priest, with its garden, old grape vine, and paved hall. Here many of the ancient records may be seen. To the north extends the cemetery, thickly beset with white crosses, where Spaniards, Mexicans, and Indians await the resurrection.

Opposite the Mission building is the old Mission garden, with the oldest vines, orange, olive, and pomegranate trees in the country. Formerly there were two lofty date palms here. One was destroyed by some

INTERIOR OF THE SAN GABRIEL MISSION.

vandal years ago, but the other stands as a monument
to the olden days.   Up the street from the Mission are
some peculiar adobe buildings, falling to decay, supposed to have been guard-houses in which drunken
Indians were confined.   To the east of the Mission,
one may still see remnants of the old *tuna* or cactus
hedge that originally inclosed effectually the Mission
and its grounds.

Those parts still extant show what a formidable
chevaux de frise this was, presenting a front of spines
from ten to fifteen feet in height.   The cactus is the
large variety known as the " Prickly Pear," and plants
from it may be seen in Pasadena, about The Raymond,
and in many towns.

All the Mission grapes in Southern California probably came from the " Mother Vineyard " here.   The
vines were dug up and carried off to various parts of
the state, and on the old road leading through it the
holes from which the huge roots were taken can be
plainly seen.

Life in San Gabriel among the Mexicans passes in
easy indifference ; they have little or no interest in
American affairs, and existence seems a continuous
season of *dolce far niente*.   The men dash up the narrow
street on their well-bred horses, and sit the day long
smoking and talking, and are, according to some rea-
soners, true philosophers, who succeed in obtaining a
vast amount of comfort from life at a minimum display
of exertion.

HISTORY OF THE MISSION.

The rise and fall of the San Gabriel Mission in years
to come will occupy an important page in the early
history of Southern California, and the events of its

growth to a powerful centre and its subsequent decay
are tinged with romance and highly exciting episodes,
secular and ecclesiastical.

In the 18th century the revolt against the powerful
order of Jesuits was consummated, and the priests and
workers were driven from Spain and forced to relinquish their authority in all her provinces. They had
obtained a firm foot-hold in Lower California, established many missions, and added to their power in
every way; but by the edict of the home government
the result of seventy years' labor was turned over to
the Franciscans, and the Jesuit missions became tribu-
tary to the friars of the College of San Fernando,
Mexico, who were then governed by Father Junipero
Serra. From their predecessors the Franciscans
learned much about Upper California; while the logs
of Cabrillo and Viscayno gave them minute information regarding the possibilities of establishing the
Church in the little known land, from San Diego to
Monterey, and finally it was determined to found
three missions — one at San Diego, one at Monterey (or
where these cities now stand), and another at some
intermediate location, to be determined later. In per-
suance of this plan, two expeditions were planned — one
to proceed over land, and the other by water, under
the command of the Father President and *Visitador
General*, appointed by the king. Three ships were
loaded with seeds and various implements needed in
the establishment of a community, and the overland
train drove cattle. With the exception of one ship, the
San Jose, they reached San Diego Bay in safety, and
on July 16, 1769, the mission of San Diego was founded.
The Monterey Mission was established in 1770, fol-

lowed by San Antonio, a short distance away, in 1771.

The success which attended these efforts was so encouraging, that a fourth mission was decided upon, the present site of San Gabriel was selected, and the following account is abridged from the life of Chief Missionary Father Junipero Serra, written by Father Palon in Mexico 1787: "On the 10th of August, 1771," says Father Palon, "the Father Prior Pedro Cambon and Father Angel Somera, guarded by ten soldiers, with the muleteers and beasts requisite to carry the necessaries, set out from San Diego, and traveled northward by the same route as the former expedition for Monterey had gone. After proceeding about forty leagues, they arrived at the river called *Temblores;* and while they were in the act of examining the ground, in order to fix a proper place for the Mission, a multitude of Indians presented themselves, setting up horrid yells, and seemed determined to oppose the establishment of the Mission.

"The fathers, fearing that war would ensue, took out a piece of cloth having thereon the image of Our Lady de los Dolores, and held it up to the view of the barbarians. This was no sooner done than the whole were quiet, being subdued by the sight of this most precious image. . . .

"They then informed the whole of the neighborhood of what had taken place ; and the people in large numbers — men, women, and children — soon came to see the Holy Virgin, bringing food which they put before her, thinking she required to eat as others. In this way the gentiles of the Mission of San Gabriel were so entirely changed that they frequented the establishment without reserve, and hardly knew how much to express their pleasure that the Spaniards had come to settle in their country.

"Under these favorable auspices the fathers proceeded to found the Mission with the accustomed ceremonies, and celebrated the first mass under a tree on the Nativity of the Virgin, the 8th day of September, 1771."

The object of the Franciscans was to convert the Indians, and this they undoubtedly did in many cases. But the establishment of the Mission was the death-knell of the race, and to-day, one hundred and seven years later, the pure-blooded Indian is a *rara avis;* so it is a question whether the conversion that results in extinction is altogether desirable.

When the good fathers entered the limits of what is now Los Angeles County, they found about forty villages, each of which was under the control of an hereditary governor or chief. Their religious belief would satisfy nine people out of ten to-day. They believed in one God, and, instead of appealing to him by name, referred to his many attributes. Every village had a circular wicker-work church. The habits of these people were simple. They used stone implements ; mortars, pestles, etc. Their money consisted of round pieces of shell, twenty-four feet of which was equal to about a dollar, so that their coinage was as cumbersome as that represented by the trade-dollar of the Americans. Despite their alleged war-like demonstrations, they were probably a peaceful people, easily influenced by their white masters, and were undoubtedly utilized by them in the work of building up the Mission. Indeed, some writers do not hesitate to say that the Indians were

little less than slaves, and in the sixty years of Franciscan domination they became dissolute, helpless, and
dependent, to such an extent that their extinction as a
race was but a matter of time.

The first Mission building, or " Mission Vieja, "
was built on a picturesque slope near the river San
Gabriel, near a well-wooded trail, and where the rush
of waters could be heard winter and summer. As to
the experiences of the founders little is known. The
Mission must have resembled the old one at Santa Fè.
Its walls were of mud or adobe, held in shape at first
by boards, while at intervals were blocks of wood to
strengthen it.

This rude building was used until about 1791, when
it was given up and another Mission established five
miles northwest, in the direction of what is now Pasadena. The reasons for this move can hardly be appreciated to-day. One was that the building was considered unsafe by reason of earthquakes, and the other
that the position was too exposed, rendering the
Mission liable to the attacks of war-like Indians. The
location of the " old Mission " is still to be recognized
by the adobe ruins of the church that surmount a hill
in the midst of a rambling Mexican village.

After much discussion the second Mission church
was established, about twelve hundred feet north of
the present San Gabriel Mission. It was far more pre-
tentious than the first one ; was of adobe, and had eight
pillars of brick, and arches of graceful form and design.

Earthquakes, which are rarely if ever experienced
here now, rendered this building defective. This, with
the largely increasing flock demanding more room,

necessitated a still larger edifice, and as a result the third and existing mission was erected in 1804.

This building, which is of rather a gloomy aspect, intended as a defence as well as a church, is long and narrow, and built of stone, with ten brick-plastered buttresses, giving it great strength. The belfry is to the west, pierced for six bells, and is picturesque and rather artistic in design. To the east end an outside staircase of stone leads to the galleries.

The original roof was of tiling, and much more tasteful than the present one; but the red tiles laid over and over made so heavy a weight that about twenty years ago they were removed and plain shingles substituted. Various buildings were built at the time, notably two mills, one of which is of great interest and will be referred to later on. About the new Mission, gardens were planted, and, with hundreds of Indians to do the work, soon a large, valuable, and influential settlement was established. Several fathers had the charge, but while under Padre Jose Maria Salvadea it attained its highest perfection as an agricultural district and a centre of ecclesiastical power.

He systematized everything, and planted trees of all kinds, recognizing the wonderful productive nature of the soil. The "Mother Vineyard," consisting of three thousand vines, was increased to over one hundred and fifty thousand. He planted the first orange trees in America on this spot, in about 1820, and they came into bearing when the first Los Angeles orchard was established in 1834. The gardens in those days presented a most delightful appearance. The vineyards were intersected with walks. Pomegranate trees formed divisional hedges. Roses were also made to do hedge-duty, and a wealth of verdure sprang up in the village. About the gardens, vineyards, orange and olive groves was planted the huge cactus fence, portions of which are still standing, and to which reference has already been made.

According to Hugo Reid, " The people were divided into classes and vocations. These included soapmakers, tanners, shoemakers, carpenters, blacksmiths, bakers, cooks, brick and tile makers, musicians, tallow-melters, pigeon-tenders, saddle-makers, deer and sheep-skin dressers, people of all work — everything but coopers ; these were foreign, all the rest being native Indians.

" Large soap-works were erected, tanning-yards established, tallow-works, and shops of various kinds, large spinning-rooms, where might be seen fifty or sixty women, turning their spindles merrily, and looms for weaving wool, flax, and cotton. . . .

" A principal head (major-domo) commanded and superintended over all. Claudio Lopez was the famed one during Padre Salvadea's administration, and, although only executing the priests' plans, in the minds of the people he is the real hero. . . . There were a great many major-domos under him for all kinds of work, from tending horses down to those superintending crops, and in charge of vineyards and gardens. . . . The best looking youths were kept as pages to attend table, and those of most musical talent were reserved for church service."

The manner of living in these good old times at the San Gabriel Mission is best told by the following bill of fare.

FIRST COURSE.
Caldo.
Plain broth, in which meat and vegetables have been boiled.)

SECOND COURSE.
La Olla.
(Boiled meats.)

THIRD COURSE.
Al Bondigas.
(Forced meat balls, in gravy.)

FOURTH COURSE.
Guisados.
(Stews — generally two.)

FIFTH COURSE.
Azado.
(Roast beef, mutton, game, fowls.)

SIXTH COURSE.
(Fruit and Sweetmeats.)

SEVENTH COURSE.
(Tea, coffee, cigarritos.)

Different wines were served with this, and, if tne old fathers were not epicures, indeed monarchs in their way, they fell little short of it.

Father Salvadea's ambition was to make the Mission the most powerful and beautiful in the country ; but unfortunately there is even in the church envy and jealousy, and suddenly the good padre was ordered to San Juan Capistrano by his superior, where he pined away, lost his reason, and finally died, a victim to envy, as it was his intellect, his master-mind, that conceived and carried out the great works. Salvadea was a ripe scholar. He was the first Spaniard who acquired the Indian language. He formulated a grammar, translated the church service into their tongue, and preached to them in the Mission chapel in their own language — a practice that was not kept up after his removal.

A glance at the old ranch, as one rides through, tells but indifferently the story of its former productiveness. As late as 1831, a season's produce was at a very low estimate as follows : Wheat, 3,500 bushels; corn, 1,000 bushels; frixol, 32.5 ; beans, 62.5 ; total, 4,595 bushels. The domestic animals belonging to the Mission were : Cattle, one hundred thousand ; horses, four thousand ; mules, one thousand ; swine, one thousand. Besides this, the Mission possessed large bands of wild horses and other possessions of great value. They owned in reality the entire country, and the twenty-one missions which were founded as follows were but points of vantage, forts armed with ecclesiastical guns and spiritual powder : —

MISSIONS OF CALIFORNIA.

Date of founding, and population in 1803, as given by Von Humboldt:

		Males.	Females.	Total.
1769	San Diego	737	822	1,559
1770	San Carlos (Carmelo).	376	312	688
1771	San Gabriel.	532	515	1,047
1771	San Antonio de Padua. .	568	484	1,052
1772	San Luis Obispo. . .	374	325	699
1776	San Juan Capistrano .	502	511	1,013
1776	San Francisco. .	433	381	814
1777	Santa Clara. . .	736	555	1,291
1782	San Buenaventura . .	436	502	938
1786	Santa Barbara. . . .	521	572	1,093
1787	La Purisima Concepcion .	457	571	1,028
1791	Soledad	296	267	563
1794	Santa Cruz . .	238	199	437
1797	San Jose. . .	327	295	622
1797	San Miguel . . .	309	305	614
1797	San Fernando.	317	297	614
1797	San Juan Bautista . .	530	428	958
1798	San Luis Rey Francia. .	256	276	532
		7,945	7,617	15,562

The Spanish government laid out certain rules which the missionaries were supposed to follow. Thus, ten years after the founding of a mission, it was to become a *pueblo*, or town, and the property taken originally by the Mission was, after the modern communistic plan, to be divided up among the natives, who, it was assumed, were now good Catholics, and capable of living like Spaniards. But the missions had become too valuable, the Indians were looked upon as brutes, and it became the policy of the missionaries (though Catholics will deny this) to give the Indians just information enough, not too much. So, in reality they were little less than slaves, and, being supported in this way, they became year by year more and more dependent.

The friars were their absolute masters, and up to 1822 they governed the work here like kings. In that year Mexico threw off the yoke of allegiance, and persons envious of the right royal life lived by the padres began to inquire why the *pueblos* had not formed, and the property been divided up. After much controversy, laws were passed declaring the Indians free, and putting certain limitations upon the power of the padres.

As an experiment, San Juan Capistrano, about thirty miles away, was constituted a village, but it was too late. Suddenly deprived of their masters, accountable to no one, the Indians seemed utterly unable to control themselves, and fell into such habits of drunkenness and vice that in less than twelve months the lawmakers saw their mistake, and the decree was repealed, so that the padres again assumed the role of masters. Still, the outcry against the missions continued. "How is it," asked inquisitive statesmen of the home govern-

ment, "that these Franciscans who profess poverty,
and who claim to be followers of Saint Francis, who
'repudiated all idea of poverty,' live like princes?"
This question was difficult to answer, and the Franciscan fathers went on improving the place, and growing
richer and richer every year, until finally in 1834 envy
and jealousy found its voice in an order from the government which resulted in the secularization of the
missions. The charge was made that the priests were
so taken up with agriculture that the spiritual welfare
of the Indians was altogether forgotten. So it came
that the missionaries were relieved from the administration of temporalities, and instructed to devote themselves more to matters of their calling. It need hardly
be said that the friars did not give up their work without a struggle. For sixty-four years their order had
labored to perfect the Mission and its ranches, and
now to relinquish all to a colony sent from Mexico
was too much, and, according to certain authorities,
they did resist. It is said that much of the work was
destroyed, vast herds of cattle killed, groves cut down,
and buildings demolished. It is only just to say that
this has been denied, though many believe that the
Franciscans preferred to see their place destroyed
rather than have it fall into the hands of strangers. In
1840 most of the buildings were, according to Hon.
B. D. Wilson, in good condition; but since then the
Church has shown little if any attempt to keep up the
place, and so it has gone to decay. The Indians, —
where are they? This will be an interesting question
for the tourist to solve. A few old people still linger
around the Mission, but the larger number have died
out or are represented by scattering bands down in

the mountains at Pauma, Pachanga, and Cahuilla. To them conversion meant extinction.

OLD RANCHES.

In driving to the Mission a number of old ranches are passed which are well worthy a visit. Near The Raymond is Los Robles (The Oaks), the ranch of Governor Stoneman, which embraces about four hundred acres, nearly all under cultivation. The vineyard which stretches away on either side of the drive produces about eight hundred tons of Mission grapes per year, or four tons per acre. The orange trees are of the seedling variety, and are about seventeen years old. The water is equivalent to fifty miner's inches, and comes from springs up the little cañon.

Next to the Stoneman place just across the little arroyo, over a wooden bridge, is the Hutchinson ranch, interesting as being one of the very old ones. Here are many curious Indian relics that have been dug up on the place, and some fine specimens of cork trees. They are forty feet in height, and about seven feet in circumference at the surface. It is the bark of this tree that affords the cork of commerce. When the trees are from twelve to fifteen years old, the cork or bark is stripped off once in six or eight years. On this ranch, a part of which was a Mission garden, are some grape vines estimated at eighty-five years old. The vines still yield bountifully, but differ to some extent from the Mission variety. Sixty pounds are still taken from single small vines. The grapes are almost seedless, — within one of it, — literally possessing but one seed each.

EL MOLINO.

To the north of this ranch, reached by a drive
through a fine grove of English walnuts, stands one
of the ancient landmarks of the Mission days — the
old mill under the bluff, overshadowed by ancient
willows, with live oaks near at hand, and a wealth of
semi-tropical fruits and flowers.   Here among singing
pines nestled in a cool retreat, an ideal spot, stands
El Molino, or the old mill, one of the most romantic
spots in the neighborhood; and sitting beneath the
great pines, listening to their soft musical murmur rising and falling on the breeze, one can give full play to
the imagination.

As to the age of El Molino, no one knows, and there
is no exact record of its builders; so in a way it is as
mysterious as the mill in Newport, R. I.   The mill
was probably built by the old friars, either at the time
of the old Mission or the existing one.   In 1859 Colonel
E. J. C. Kewen bought it, and, after improving the place,
established his home there.   The building then, as
near as can be determined, was exactly as it was originally, and many of the trees about the place were
planted by the old fathers.

At this time the building was fifty-five feet long and
twenty-four feet broad.   So heavy and solid is it, that
it might have been intended as a fort; the walls are
heavy and ponderous, and by actual measurement six
feet thick.

The room made into a parlor by the last occupant
had two small deep windows, protected by iron bars
and heavy wooden shutters, showing that the builders,
whoever they were, considered that protection was

necessary; and as to the strength and durability of the wall we are informed by Alice P. Adams that to enlarge these windows to a modern size required a man forty days, or twenty days to a window.

The mill stands at the entrance of a little cañon, and on the eastern side we see the two large arches in which the mill machinery was supported, and where the huge wheel revolved. Here Colonel Kewen added a room, so that the general appearance is changed to some extent. The lower side of the building is marked by two large buttresses of conical shape, built of stone, and decorated or covered with a coating of cement.

From beneath one of the buttresses flows a single stream of water, probably coming from a spring. The flow, according to the people who have lived in the vicinity, has not diminished for thirty years, despite dry and unfavorable seasons, probably finding its source far below the surface. The spring now flows into or forms a pool, surrounded by callas, whose luxuriance has become a proverb. Over five hundred have been picked at one time without entirely depleting the supply. It is told of an Eastern lady who came to Southern California in January, in breaking up her home in the East, a calla, that had been nursed through many a winter, was preserved and brought in the cars with the greatest care. The lady's friends met her at San Gabriel, and on the way to Pasadena jokingly took her to see the callas of El Molino, when it is said that the petted flower was cast aside.

Originally the roof of the mill was of tiling; but it proved a famous camping-ground for rats, bats, skunks, and owls, so they were finally replaced by shingles.

The old mill, which is going to decay again, is the property of the Mayberry estate, and I believe the building
is unoccupied. The flowers are neglected, rose bushes
have run wild, and the adobe structure in the near
vicinity, used by Colonel Kewen as a billiard-room, is
given over to the " Heathen Chinee."

A ride to El Molino on a moonlight night in summer is a delightful experience. The moonbeams
streaming down through the willow branches form fantastic figures ; the mournful note of the wood dove
comes softly; great bats dart noiselessly about, and
far up the little cañon we may hear mayhaps the cry
of the wild-cat or coyote. The stream splashes gently,
and the callas about the old fountain, neglected and
overgrown, gleam like phantoms. Never was a place
better adapted for ghosts ; and, if some sad-eyed, fair-
haired woman is not seen walking about, or the clanking of chains occasionally heard, it is because the
romancers have not done their duty.

THE WILSON RANCH.

Adjoining the mill property is the old Lake Vineyard ranch, the property of the heirs of the late Hon.
B. D. Wilson. He purchased the property from Hugo
Reid in 1852. It was then very much as the Mission
Fathers had left it. There were some ancient orange,
pear, and olive trees, twenty thousand vines, and an
extensive peach orchard, through the centre of which
extended a broad avenue with a double row of pomegranate trees, which, with their richly colored flowers,
presented a magnificent appearance. Originally this
road led to the lake, and the entire orchard was

inclosed by an adobe wall ; the latter was taken down some years ago, and the estate planted with vines.

The Wilson homestead is a large, roomy house, of brick and adobe, costing in 1854 about $20,000, nearly half of which, according to Miss Adams, was spent on the roof. Beneath the house is a large wine cellar. Mr. Wilson was a man of great intelligence, and the pioneer of all the improvements of the day. He planted the second orange grove in San Gabriel. Wilson's Peak, the highest mountain in the vicinity, bears his name, and he built the trail now in use up the mountain, his object being to obtain lumber for barrel-staves. The trail cost $6,000, and every stave was brought down on a burro.

In the estimation of the writer, the most delightful region about Pasadena is the old Wilson estate. It is now known as Wilson's pasture, and has against all reason been sold in acre lots. It is a natural park of the most beautiful description, and should have been preserved as one. There are several small cañons of surpassing beauty, groves of live oak, — many of the trees giants, overhung with wild grape, — huge sycamores, on whose branches the great California condor rests, and fine level stretches ; in all embodying all the requisites of a fine park. Wilson's cañon and pasture are now fenced in, but permission can be obtained to drive through ; and this choice spot, blooming with flowers in mid-winter, should not be neglected in strolls about Pasadena. Near here is San Morino, the home of J. De Barth Shorb, Esq., son-in-law of Mr. Wilson. The attractive Mission Cañon divides the properties, and here springs the stream that provides San Gabriel Mission with its water. From the front of San Morino a view of great beauty is seen, especially in the direction of Puente and the valley. This imposing mansion is surrounded by a wealth of tropical vegetation, sago, fan and other palms, and is one of the finest residences in Southern California.

Near at hand is the Cooper ranch, of interest as being the pear orchard of the old Mission Fathers. Here are two fine palms brought from the desert thirty years ago, now tall, bulky, and picturesque. From this ridge we look to the south and east over the land of the old friars; a fairer country it would be difficult to find. Here is material for the romancer and historian. Here lived a powerful and prolific native race not two hundred years ago. The story of its disappearance is an impressive one — like the buffalo and various other animals, they have been swept away by the resistless, onward wave of human progress.

CHAPTER VII.

THE ANCIENT PASADENIANS.

Sites of ancient villages. Curious stone implements unearthed. Stone mortars and pestles. Arrow heads, Matates, Discoidal stones. The discoverer of Los Angeles County.

IN driving about Pasadena the visitor will see in a number of places curious stones hollowed out, well-rounded stone clubs, flat-faced grinding stones, and a variety of rude stone implements evidently of great age.

These objects have been plowed up in various parts of the city, and represent the household gods of the aboriginal Pasadenian, the dishes, grain crushers, balls for playing games, and weapons of a people about which very little is known.

Before referring to them it will perhaps interest the reader to read portions of a diary or log of Jean Rodriguez Cabrillo, a Spanish adventurer, who was the first white man to enter San Pedro, the port of entry of Los Angeles County.

The voyage was made in 1542, three hundred and forty-six years ago — one hundred years after the discovery of America by Columbus. The record was found in a library in Madrid : —

"On the Tuesday and Wednesday following they sailed along the coast about eight leagues, and passed by some three uninhabited islands (probably Catalina and San Clemente). One of them was larger than the other and extended two entire leagues, and forms a shelter

from the west winds. They are three leagues from
the main land; they are in thirty-four degrees. This
day they saw on land great signal smokes. It is a
good land in appearance, and there are great valleys,
and in the interior there are high ridges. They called
them Las Islas Desiertas (the desert isles).

"The Thursday following they proceeded about six
leagues by a coast running north, northwest, and discovered a port inclosed, and very good, to which they
gave the name of San Miguel (San Pedro Harbor). It is
in thirty-four and a third degrees, and after anchoring in
it they went ashore, which had people, three of whom
remained and all the others fled. To these they
gave some presents, and they said by signs that in
the interior had passed people like the Spaniards.
They manifested much fear. The next morning they
entered farther into the port, and brought away
two boys, who understood nothing by signs, and
they gave them both shirts, and immediately sent
them away. And the following morning there came
to the ship three large Indians, and by signs they
said that there were traveling in the interior men like
us, with beards, and clothed and armed like those of
the ships . . . . This people (the natives) were well
disposed and advanced; they go covered with skins
of animals."

To show how well populated the coast was, the following from the same narrative is given : —

"On the Sunday following the 15th day of the same
month they held on their voyage along the coast about
ten leagues, and there were always many canoes, for
all the coast is very populous, and many Indians were
continually coming aboard the ships ; and they pointed

out to us the villages and named them by their names,
which are Xucu, Bis, Sopono, Alloc, Xataagua, Xot-
ococ, Potoltuc, Nacbuc, Quelqueme, Misinagua, Elquis,
Coloc, Mugu, Xagua, Anacbuc, Partocac, and many
more.   All these villages extended from the first pueblo
de las canoas; . . . . they are in a very good country,
with many good trees and cabins ; the natives go
clothed in skins, and they said that inland were many
towns and much maize at three days' distance."

The trip or voyage extended well north, and the
account shows that the entire California country was
well settled ; that the coast was built up with villages,
and that the natives stated that the interior was also
densely populated.   The men in the interior, to which
they referred as having beards, were evidently men
belonging to Coronado's party.

These people were undoubtedly the ancestors of the
Indians found there by the Franciscan fathers.

In 1852 a report was made by the Hon. B. D. Wilson
to the Department of the Interior, to the effect that
there were then in Santa Barbara, Tulare, Los Angeles,
and San Diego Counties about fifteen thousand
Indians, comprising the Tulareños, Cahuillas, San Luis-
enos, and Diegaenos.   Thirty years later another report
was made showing a decrease of ten thousand; the
remaining five thousand are fast disappearing.

The writer has visited many of their villages, especially at Pala, Pauma, Temecula, Pachanga, and
San Jacinto, and very few full-blooded Indians are left.
Nearly all have inter-married with Mexicans, Americans,
or Negroes.   They live in the tule huts, some in adobe:
the men going around the country, working on the
big ranches.   They wear American clothes, but, as a

rule, are a sorry lot, morally and mentally. In the huts I invariably found the old stone mortar and pestle of their forefathers. In answer to inquiries, they replied that they did not make them, but found them in the fields. The introduction of modern utensils has rendered useless, to a great extent, the huge mortars, and they are probably not made at present. In some huts they were utilized to feed chickens from. In others grain was still ground, and on all the ranches where they are dug up, they serve for various purposes, either in the pig-corral, or elsewhere.

The writer has a collection of twenty or more of these mortars, most of which were found upon the slopes of the mountains in San Diego County. They range in weight from two hundred and seventy-nine pounds to two pounds, the smaller ones evidently having been used by children.

The San Gabriel Valley was once dotted with these Indian villages, and five and six hundred years ago was undoubtedly the centre of a strong and powerful race.

That Pasadena's delightful location was recognized, we have every reason to believe, as in hundreds of localities implements have been found, telling the interesting story of the occupation of an almost forgotten and lost race.

The natives generally located their towns or settlements where there was a good water supply, and if possible on a hill or elevated situation. The Giddings' ranch is the site of an extremely old settlement; and for years objects of various kinds, mostly old and broken, have been plowed up. They were generally flat, shallow mortars, of a dark stone, with short, flat grinding or mealing stones. In following the plow of Mr. Giddings I have seen pieces of mortars or pestles thrown up every few moments, showing that large numbers must have been left here; and, as they are buried a foot or more below the surface, it is evident that they are older than many others found upon the surface. The old town was situated at what is now the beginning of the road leading down into Millard Cañon; and the assumption is that the women went into the cañon to collect acorns, which were brought down to the village to be ground. Every year at plowing time, which comes between November and Christmas, specimens are unearthed.

Another Indian village was situated on what is now the Orange Grove Avenue Reservoir, east of Park Place. When the earth was removed, large numbers of mortars, pestles, mealing and other stones were discovered, and after a heavy rain we may still pick up the flat grinding-stones in the immediate vicinity.

On the San Rafael ranch, opposite the west end of California Street, many interesting specimens have been found, and the author has picked them up in various parts of the city. Few of the older residents but possess a collection of some size.

The most valuable collection belongs to H. N. Rust, Esq., of South Pasadena. Mr. Rust is an enthusiastic archæologist, and possesses a cabinet valued at many thousands of dollars. Here are complete sets of mortars and pestles, ranging in size from those weighing two or three hundred pounds to the smallest paint pots, discoidal stones, plummets, daggers, arrow heads, flint chips, basket-work — in fact, almost every article used by these ancient people can be seen here. Not only

is the collection rich in specimens relating to Southern
California, but it contains objects from Arizona, New
and Old Mexico, dishes made and used by the old
mound builders, and a variety of implements of the
greatest beauty and value. The collection as a whole
has not its equal in the West; and a view of it, which,
by the courtesy of its owner, is often possible, tells the
story of the ancient Californians at a glance.

Around the attractive grounds of Mr. Rust are many
curious and interesting specimens — huge mortars,
weighing over two hundred pounds, roughly-hewn mortars, mealing-stones, and other specimens from all over
Southern California.   .

In olden times baskets constituted an important
feature of the domestic life of the natives, and they
are still used to a greater or less extent. These baskets
exceed in beauty of color and finish any made by the
Eastern Indians; many are works of art, and artistic
in every sense of the word, both in shape and color.
The baskets are made of native grasses of various
kinds, often woven in a beautiful manner, and so
closely that they will hold water.

The basket-maker may be seen at San Gabriel, where
the grand-daughter of *Laura*, who recently died at the
ripe old age of one hundred and seventeen years, still
carries on the basket-making business.

The baskets of the southern Indians are, as a rule,
coarse, while those from Tulare and the north are
finer, and more elegant. The latter are often ornamented richly with beads and feathers ; and the old
ones, that with age have assumed a rich brown hue,
bring large prices from connoisseurs ; fifty, seventy-
five, and even one hundred dollars having been paid

for artistic shapes. So beautiful are these baskets, and so well adapted for interior and artistic decoration, that they have been bought up from the old Mexican families and Indians wherever obtainable, so that now all the old baskets are in private collections. Several hundred baskets could probably be collected in Pasadena, representing hundreds of dollars. Mr. Rust has a fine collection, one having especial interest, as having been given him by " H. H." when on her trip through the country, obtaining material for " Ramona." It might be stated in this connection that Mrs. Jackson obtained the name " Ramona " from Mrs. J. De Barth Shorb, who possesses it. It is often said that she first heard the name at Mrs. Ramona Wolfs', at Temecula, but the former statement is probably correct.

The history of this country is replete with interest, and those sojourning here will find it a profitable study. The Pasadena Library contains many books relating to the subject ; and the historical works of Hubert H. Bancroft of San Francisco contain everything available. The following books have references to the early discovery of the country : " Explorations in Lower California," Brown ; " History of California," Capron ; " Life and Adventures in California," Farnham ; " Fuguet, La California," " Oregon and California," Greenhow ; De Morpas' " Explorations." The volume of the " Geographical Survey of the One Hundredth Meridian," on archæology, contains many illustrated papers of interest on this country and a complete list of papers referring to it.

CHAPTER VIII.

PASADENA AS A HEALTH RESORT

Compared to Italy, France, Florida, St. Paul, and Colorado. The climate. A challenge to the world.

PASADENA has been so much talked of, written about abroad, and described by so many enthusiasts, that it is not singular that it has been placed too high upon the scale of excellence. People who have left snow-banks in the East, and in a few days find themselves among Pasadena's gardens, invalids who have come here without hope and have recovered, naturally extol the place to the highest, and interlard their descriptions with the term " Paradise," etc.

Pasadena does not profess to be a Paradise or a modern Garden of Eden. Its claim is simply that in its climate, scenery, and general conditions it has the essentials that make it the finest health resort in this country or Europe. The tourist who lands at The Raymond in a rain storm and leaves in three or four days, after having part of each day rainy, or the man or woman who came too late to be cured, naturally doubt this ; but, while the statement is a broad one, it can be easily verified.

Pasadena cannot be sampled like its wine ; cannot be tested by the aroma or odor of one orange tree. The test is a comparison by the year, from January to January, with other famous health resorts of the world.

It is conceded by medical men of all schools that lung troubles cannot be eradicated in a few months.

In other words, where doctors ten years ago said "take a sea voyage, or a few weeks in the Adirondacks or in Florida," they now advise the invalid to go to some locality and live for several years, enjoy an out-of-door life and an entire change of habits. Can this advice be followed to advantage in Florida? The writer, who has lived in the land of flowers winter and summer for five or six years, thinks not. The Florida season is from November to April, and during this time is delightful, yet much of it is malarious. The invalid has a few months to recuperate, and then must return North to avoid the debilitating heat, insect pests, malaria, and possibly yellow fever; in other words, few people prefer to summer in Florida if they can get away, and it is not recommended as a summer health resort.

The Adirondacks are delightful in summer, and I can conceive of no more fascinating place than Alexandria Bay; yet a winter in these places is not a pleasant outlook for one delicate and ordered to live out of doors. At St. Paul the winters are intensely cold, the summers hot. At Colorado Springs, where the writer has lived, we have an altitude something like the top of Mount Washington, cold winters and intensely hot summers, with almost daily rain storms with accompanying thunder and lightning. The climate is dry and bracing.

In the famous Rivièra of Italy and Southern France we have mild winters and a delightful season from November to April; then come debilitating hot winds from the African coast, and the famous resorts are given over to malarial troubles.

Pasadena, on the other hand, offers what none of

these possess — a delightful climate from one end of the year to the other. The invalid can live here far more comfortably than elsewhere every month in the year. There is no going north or south in the different seasons; you may change your altitude six thousand feet in four or five hours, or attain the summit of the Sierra Madres, or the sea level, as you wish.

If in Florida you were ordered to change your altitude, it would be a matter of days of travel, and probably there are no hotels in the mountains of Tennessee, where you would go. Here, a series of hotels range from the Pacific to the base of the mountains, to four thousand feet above it; and the extremes of the change, as an example, from the Hotel Arcadia, on the coast, to Switzer's, north of Pasadena, can be made in less than a day.

The seasons here are a puzzle to the new-comer. They are termed the wet and the dry — terms that convey an erroneous impression, as the rainy season is not more rainy than an eastern summer, and by means of irrigation the dry season can be made as wet as desirable. The dry season is the time when it is not supposed to rain, but sometimes does; this includes the months from April to November. The wet season, or winter, is from November to April or May, when it rains perhaps once in three weeks, sometimes oftener, and sometimes not so often, the seasons changing in this respect just as they change in the East. The amount of rain at Pasadena may be averaged at twenty inches, thirty-five less than at Jacksonville and twenty-nine less than Boston; so the wet season is by no means a deluge. The winter at Pasadena may be compared to a cool eastern fall.

In October the weather grows slightly cooler, and
soon the rains come. This gives renewed life to all
vegetation, and instead of frost, snow, and ice, the
land blooms like a garden, the *mesas* are carpeted with
a succession of flowers, the low hills take on a vivid
green tint, and the air is filled with fragrant odors.
The birds driven from the north throng the groves
and meadows, and by Christmas time Pasadena is in
the midst of what appears, as far as nature, fruits, and
flowers are concerned, mid-summer. The mountain
tops are covered with snow, sometimes reaching down
to within a thousand feet of the orange trees. But so
subtle are the conditions that, though we see winter
and summer face to face, scarce half a mile apart,
yet there is little or no encroachment. Occasionally
on rare occasions ice forms in pools in Pasadena, and
frost is seen. The evening will seem cold and chilly,
and a fire on the hearth is very acceptable ; indeed,
many persons have a fire morning and evening
throughout the winter. As you sit by your fire the
wind may sweep down, howl, and rage. You hear it
under the eaves. How cold it sounds! and you move
nearer the fire. Surely a snow blizzard is in progress.
You go to the door. The thermometer indicates sixty
degrees, and you find it was a Gold of Ophir rose
beating against the window, and the rustling of the
palm leaves carries out the impression of the storm.
When the mercury indicates freezing, it seems exces-
sively cold by contrast ; yet how cold the weather in
Pasadena really is, is shown by the fact that the roses,
callas, and all flowers, wild and otherwise, bloom
throughout the entire winter ; if they live, the cold
cannot be intense.

The touch of cold weather in the winter is bracing
and extremely beneficial.   It gives some change
between winter and summer; yet, as slight as is the
cold, fault is often found with it.   But Pasadena does
not claim to be a tropical climate; it is a moderate or
semi-tropical one, only tropical in that palms, bananas,
pomegranates, and other southern plants grow here
winter and summer out of doors.   You are offered
a winter where the flowers bloom, where the birds
sing, with cool mornings and nights.   From six o'clock
at night to eight o'clock in the morning in winter,
Pasadena out of doors, taking an average, is like an
eastern October, where the thermometer does not, as a
rule, stray below fifty or sixty degrees.   The winter day,
from nine until five, taking an average again, is one in
which the doors may be left open.   To refer to exact
figures, the winter mean is fifty-six degrees, autumn
62.31.   Sometimes the season is unusually rainy,
again cloudy; but, as a rule, bright sunshine prevails.
The writer wishes to emphasize this point — the seasons here vary just as they do all over the world ; one
year differs from another.   As an example, the season
of 1887 was unusually cloudy, and in 1885–86 the
winters were like summers.   At its worst there are
more sunshiny out-of-door days in Pasadena than any
place in the East, and a careful record kept by the
United States Signal Service shows that in this county
there are more pleasant days in the course of the year
than in any other place in the country.   It is truly the
land of out-of-door life.

While the rainfall is amply sufficient to make the
change of season, it does not accumulate and form
malaria-producing bogs.   The nearest swamp to Pasa-

dena is at Ballona, nearly thirty miles away, and this is salt. The ground is made up mainly of disintegrating granite, so that the water almost immediately disappears. After a morning of drenching rain the afternoon will find the main drives around the city in good condition.

The visitor will miss the thunder storm, which is rarely if ever seen, though sometimes a rumble is heard over in the Sierra Madres. Sudden rains are equally rare; storms working up with great deliberation and passing away as slowly. The "signs" are the wind from the southeast and low, fleecy clouds creeping along the mountains. After a good rain it will well repay the tourist to visit the falls in the various cañons, and watch the effect of the water, as it is these winter torrents that have made the myriad cañons of the range and their many tributaries.

Pasadena has been generally referred to as a winter resort; but why it is difficult to imagine, as the summers here are as delightful as in almost any place in the East. One is never so uncomfortable as in New York, Chicago, Boston, or Philadelphia; and the writer, who has spent seasons in all the resorts in the East from the St. Lawrence to Cape May and Old Point Comfort, has found greater actual comfort in Los Angeles County. The reason for this is that here you have an actual and positive guarantee of cool nights; so cool that in riding at night a light overcoat is needed by a not over-robust person. An eminent physician told the writer that Pasadena was the most remarkable place for making up lost sleep he had ever seen, and by throwing open windows and sleeping under a blanket the perfection of somnolent conditions are found.

The atmosphere is dry and bracing. At mid-day the heat may be intense, ranging sometimes from eighty to ninety degrees in the shade ; but the rule is a much lower temperature, the mean for summer being sixty-seven degrees. At nine or ten o'clock the trade wind begins to blow, a delightfully cool, refreshing breeze, and if perchance a fog has been covering the valley by night, the tincture of delicious coolness in the air is still more striking. The trade wind from the ocean blows until sundown ; not the boisterous wind of San Francisco, but a gentle wind. Between six and seven there is a lull, and then there pours down from the mountain a cool, invigorating breeze, laden with the odors of the pine and upland trees.

The entire Pacific Coast is susceptible to fogs, but in the writer's experience the fogs of Pasadena are by no means so objectionable as those at Newport, R. I. Here they come in only at night, and rarely if ever last until nine o'clock in the morning ; so, if a person were a late riser, he might live in Pasadena for a long time and not be aware that there were fogs. They are a positive benefit, cooling the heated atmosphere. Sometimes they are observed for weeks ; and in a residence of three years there we have seen but few entirely foggy days, and these would have been termed cloudy days in the East, the fog being at least a thousand feet above the surface, and not rendering objects inconspicuous.

The term " dry season " would indicate that everything was burnt up during the summer ; but such is by no means the case. Each family has a " shower " or " rain " in the place, and by turning a faucet water is obtained to any extent ; so lawns surround every house. Neither are the hills bare. True, they are not so rich

in greens as during the winter, but the live-oaks, the
sycamores, the manzanita, and various other forms are
green the year round, and wild flowers greet you in
the arroyos ; the orange, lemon, lime, and olive groves
are perennially green ; the vineyards cover miles of
country, not to speak of peach and apricot ; so that no
one would suspect that Pasadena was passing through
its dry season.   In its beauty of summer verdure it
will equal almost any eastern city.

To the invalid the out-door life is everything, winter
or summer.   One has often three hundred and forty
pleasant days that can be spent in the clear, open air.
There is an utter absence of blizzards, cyclones, and
electric storms.   In a three years' experience we
have seen only one severe wind storm, which
did some damage in exposed places.   Indeed,
when the immunity of the locality from winds,
storms, and sudden changes is considered ; when it is
compared to the heated inter-oceanic States with their
cyclones in summer and blizzards in winter ; the
Eastern States with their severe thunder storms, tem-
pests, blizzards, intense seasons of heat and sunstroke ; the South with its hot, debilitating, malaria-
producing summers, this region excites the greatest
wonder and astonishment.   It is not Paradise, as I
have said ; but a careful examination of the country
year after year will certainly justify the statement that
it possesses more in every way to make life pleasant
and less to render it uncomfortable than any one spot
that can be mentioned in this country or the available
portions of Europe.   The actual difference between
winter and summer is expressed by eleven degrees ;
so the sudden changes from summer to intense cold so

dreaded by some are not felt. Contrasted with the difference in other places, it amounts to nothing. The difference between winter and summer at St. Augustine, Fla., is twenty-two degrees; Jacksonville, Fla., twenty-six degrees; Denver, forty-four degrees; St. Paul, fifty-two degrees.

VARIETY OF CLIMATE.

It is not the climate alone that commends itself, but its great variety. Pasadena lies on an elevated valley, one thousand feet above the Pacific. On one hand is the ocean, thirty miles away, with its resorts always cool and bracing; and upon the other the great system of the Sierra Madre Mountains, giving entirely opposite conditions. So we have a range of altitude from the sea level to six thousand feet above it within reach, and attainable in a few hours; deep cañons, dry plateaus, warm mesas, the deep, cool Arroyo, the seaside resorts, giving every possible condition that one might require, except of course the absolutely dry, arid plateau — like many towns in New Mexico, Arizona, etc. It is conceded that people require something besides climate. If a patient is sent from home, and has to rough it in a mining camp or a border town with none of the luxuries or attentions to which he has been habituated, home-sickness and kindred ailments may offset the good possibly obtainable. In Pasadena one finds all the best features of Eastern towns : a refined and cultivated society, where the same conditions exist as in the East; libraries, societies, churches — in short, the visitor will probably find everything here to which he was accustomed at home, except thunder storms, blizzards, mad dogs, and sunstroke.

CHAPTER IX.

THE ROD AND THE GUN.

Available game. Quail, dove, pigeon, ducks and geese, cranes, rabbits, etc. Trout, sea-fishing, etc. Wild goat hunting.

PASADENA possesses a "Gun and Hunt" Club, the members of which are always ready to give any information to strangers regarding the available game in the country.

The club was organized to encourage legitimate sport of all kinds, from trap shooting to coursing with greyhounds or hunting the wild-cat.

Members of the club own a fine pack of greyhounds, and the Bandini fox hounds are the attraction of many meets in the Arroyo. The small game consists of quail, two varieties; the valley or *Lophortyx Californicus*, and the mountain form. The valley quail is a most beautiful little creature, with jaunty plumes which it erects as it runs along, or eyes you from some vantage ground. The sportsman from the East will find the little bird a fair test of his powers, it being an extremely rapid flyer, going like a shot when flushed.

The favorite quail-shooting grounds are along the base of the mountains, and near the entrances to the big cañons. Here they are seen in the open, often in the great washes by thousands, though in bands of from ten to fifty.

Whether dogs can be used to advantage is a question. The work is entirely different from that to which dogs are used in the East, and the spines of the cactus are a feature which they do not understand. A good retrieving dog would certainly be a benefit, as the birds have a remarkable habit of crawling into holes or crevices when shot, and of avoiding pursuit in many ways. I have found the best method, at least about Pasadena, is to move ahead quickly and take the birds as they are flushed. When in the brush, say two feet high, they are constantly moving ahead, and make remarkable progress.

Quail can almost always be met with in Altadena, near the mouth of Millard Cañon ; and a good place is in the wash of Eaton's Cañon, and the country in that vicinity. A team is required, as if game is not found in one locality it will be necessary to move on a mile or more. The foot hills of the La Cañada Valley afford good shooting, especially as they are not over worked in the season. The quail is a domestic little fellow, and oftentimes he is seen in the garden or trotting down the road in front of your horse.

Proximity to a flock is always announced by the male, who utters a sweet and curious note which may be likened to the word *po-ta-to*, with the accent on the second syllable. They have other notes also by which they are soon known.

When flushed the birds rise and are upon the instant under full headway, and they must be shot on the rise.

The mountain quail, *Orcortyx pictus*, may be said to be rare here. It is larger than its cousin of the low-lands, and the plumes are longer and more pointed, resembling quill pens thrust behind one's ear. They are found in the upper range, also in the hills back of the city, generally where there is brush near at hand.

The sportsman who bags a goodly number may consider himself fortunate.

Quail shooting here, like sport of all kinds, is often
followed or taken up merely as an excuse to be out of
doors. Mere walking about with no special aim often
tires one ; but the hunter, having some object in view,
enjoys the country all the more. A day's quail shooting, say in January or February, will be a novelty to the
sportsman direct from the East. A good team of
horses, guns and lunch, and we are off, intending to
take the foot hills from Pasadena to Monrovia and back.

The mountains are white with snow, and the air
of the valley redolent with the odor of flowers. Birds
sing in almost every bush, and soon the *po-ta-to* of the
quail is heard, perhaps in some one's orange grove,
within gunshot of The Raymond. Quail are taken,
providing you are in luck, all the way down, and coming
back in the cool of the afternoon the rabbit shooting
may generally be counted fair. Two kinds of rabbits
are found—the Jack, the long-eared leaper found so
extensively through the West, and the smaller cotton-
tail.

Hunting the Jack is fair sport, especially with the
rifle ; and some Pasadena shots take them upon the
dead run. They are found around Altadena. They
often spring up beneath your feet, and quick shooting
is required to bring them down. When hit upon the
run, they often shoot into the air two or three feet.
Jacks are found in the open, often suddenly darting
out of a patch of weed, while the cotton-tail keeps
more to cover.

In the cañons is found a fine gray squirrel, often
eyeing you from the limb of a lofty sycamore, and form-

ing good sport with the rifle. The cañons also constitute the congregating ground of the great banded
pigeon, a bird difficult to shoot, and consequently a
prize. It occasionally wanders down into the low
country; being seen in the great ranches, which, like
Baldwin's, are well wooded. The common dove also
affords good shooting. The badger is found in the low
lands or open *mesa*, though rarely seen, and the coyote's
bark is often heard at night.

The large game available is the black-tailed deer,
mountain lion, black and grizzly bear.

Mr. E. W. Giddings brought the last grizzly into
Pasadena ; but they are rarely found, only occasionally
coming down from the upper and inner range to the
lower ridges. So with the mountain lion ; one or two
are occasionally seen every winter. A large one was
shot during the winter of 1887, in the low hills below
The Raymond. It was prowling about the sheep corral.
Another was killed by a man living on the Wilson trail.
These, as well as other animals, never attack human
beings, and it can be said that about Pasadena there is
absolutely no animal that menaces one's comfort. To
obtain big game requires hard work, and regular hunts
should be organized under the charge of an experienced
guide. Elizabeth Lake can be visited in this way, and
antelope can be found in a day's trip from Pasadena
up by Tulare. The big-horned sheep has been seen
on the slopes of Old Baldy.

Deer hunting may be had in the mountains overlooking Pasadena ; and the Verdugo Hills, six or eight
miles to the northwest, afford the best ground.
Hounds and a bush beater are absolute necessities.
The sportsmen are stationed around on the peaks,

and the beater and dogs take to the cañon, and drive the deer up where the hunter can shoot them across the cañon. Such shooting requires the very best marksmanship.

The author has had some experience in the North woods of the Adirondacks and in the Canadian forests, as well as the rough countries of Virginia and Florida ; but the climb on horseback up the slope of the Verdugo Hill was a new experience.

It was "up and down work," and the only thing to do was to embrace the horse, put one's arms about his neck, and with him literally butt through the bush, manzanita, grease wood, yuccas, and various barriers stopping the way.

On an eminence not far from the top, we rested; and while here looking down into the deep abyss, rich in its tints of green, the baying of the dogs, short and fitful, told of game, and a moment later a doe broke cover, and dashed along the side of the opposite cliff. It was so far away that it appeared about the size of a large dog ; yet my companion broke its leg almost at the first fire.

The deer is the *Cariacus columbianus* of science. Its habitat is among the thick bush of the mountain slopes, winding its way in and out of the cañons and defiles, rarely being seen in the open country, except perhaps when the mountains of the inner range are covered with snow. Fair sport may be had hunting the wild goat of Catalina Island. The "wild goat" is simply the common species, running wild. It is said that they were placed upon the island years ago, to appease the appetite of possible shipwrecked sailors ; but they were probably carried over with sheep, and, not being in demand, have increased, so that there are several large bands just wild enough to constitute long-range shooting.

A good plan is to secure the services of "Mexican Joe," the genial hunter and fisherman. Horses are to be had at the Hotel Metropol, and in an hour or so you are over some romantic trails, and upon the summit of the mountains that apparently cover the island and constitute its make up. The goats are found in various places ; sometimes in Clear Water Cañon, or others are again in the open. They are decently shy, as a "domestic wild goat" should be. And viewing the wild gorges, the flying mist-clouds, the maze of mountains, the imaginative sportsman can consider the hills the Alps, and the goats chamois.

In the fall season, the duck and goose shooting between Pasadena and the sea is good. A small lake is formed in the Puente Hills, south of The Raymond, after the rains, and here, by building a cover or blind, fair shooting may be had. The Laguna ranch, over beyond, is still better ; while Ballona harbor and swamp — the latter rented by the Los Angeles Gun Club — affords the best sport of this kind.

The fishing about Pasadena is limited to the trout, found in the pools of the Arroyo and the various cañon streams. The best fishing-ground is that of the San Gabriel Cañon and its tributaries. The fish are often found in water so shallow as to seem impossible to float them. In the cañons there is little opportunity to use a fly or split bamboo-rod ; yet in the pools of the Arroyo Seco, immediately back of the city, fish of fair size have been taken with a fly.

The salt-water fishing compares favorably with that

of the East. The gamy barracuda takes the place of the bluefish, while the Spanish mackerel and several varieties of this tribe constitute good sport. Boats for fishing may be had at San Pedro, but the fisherman will do better to make Santa Catalina his headquarters.

Here in June and July the barracuda run in schools, and some days are caught by thousands; again they will not take the hook. In these months, the sea bass, a magnificent fish much resembling a salmon, fill the bays, swimming at the surface and occasionally taking the hook, but affording greater sport with the harpoon. They attain a length of three or four feet, and run up to seventy pounds weight.

A large variety of fish are caught, including a small sea bass, much resembling a black bass and quite as gamy. It must be confessed that none of these denizens of the sea have the flavor of the game fishes of the East, due in all probability to the high temperature of the water.

The bays of Catalina and the rocks of San Pedro afford the lover of nature many opportunities for investigation. Off shore the flying-fish leaps into the air and skims away; and beneath the wave are endless forms of life interesting and unknown, awaiting the investigator.

Whales are common all along shore, and occasionally the great basking shark, thirty or forty feet long, is seen, or the giant ray, ten or fifteen feet across.

The game laws of California, as recently amended, are as follows :—

Quail, partridge, grouse, rail, September 10 to March 1.

Doves, June 1 to January 1.

Male antelope, deer or bucks, July 1 to December 15.

Female antelope, elk, mountain sheep, female deer or doe, killing at any time unlawful.

Spotted fawn, killing prohibited.

Taking quail, partridge, grouse, or rail by net or pound, prohibited.

Trout, April 1 to November 1.

Salmon, October 1 to August 31.

Fishing for salmon, shad, etc., with nets, between six o'clock Saturday evening and sundown of succeeding Sunday, prohibited.

Fishing by explosives, or by pound, weir, cage, trap, or set net, prohibited.

EUCALYPTUS AND ORANGE GROVES, NEAR EATON'S CANON.

Matthews-Northrup

CHAPTER X.

Coursing with Greyhounds.   Wild-cat hunts.   Coyote hunting.   Fox hunts.

THE country in the immediate vicinity of Pasadena is a most attractive one to the equestrian, abounding, as it does, in drives and trails of singular variety and beauty.

Simple riding, however, with no object, is often tiresome; but to those who care for the pleasures of the hunt a better field cannot be presented. The upland country of Pasadena, or the *mesa*, as it is called, abounds in the Jack rabbit. It cannot be found in droves, as in the country farther north, but in sufficient numbers to provide the experienced horseman or woman with an abundance of sport.

From one to four greyhounds and good horses constitute the necessary " out-fit " for an afternoon's outing. The party, following Marengo Avenue, soon mount Monk Hill, or Washington Heights, as it is now called. That next to the Raymond Hill is the highest prominence in the city. From here there is a fine view of the valley, and the mountains seem to be within almost reaching distance.

The country to the northeast, in the direction of Eaton's Cañon, appears to be depressed, rising to Altadena, and stretching away toward the cañon, dotted with villas and ranches. Here in the *chaparral*, the Jack rabbit holds forth, as well as its small cousin the cotton-tail.

The morning and evening, or rather the cooler portions of the day, are best adapted for the sport. The
dogs present an attractive appearance, their long, lithe
forms seemingly built for speed and endurance. They
spread out and cover the field, move on for a few yards,
then stop and look about unless instructed to beat the
bush for game ; but the slow approach is the best, as
in this case the " Jack " does not move until the dogs
are fairly upon it.

Perhaps a mile of the field has been covered; ladies
and gentlemen are gayly chatting, when suddenly from
beneath the horses' feet dashes a small object with long,
black-tipped ears. He appears to shoot from the brush
into the air, and in a second the dogs and horses are
in full chase. There is not a sound save the rush of
feet, as the dogs are silent ; but the lack of music is
amply compensated for by the fine display of running.
At first the dogs appear to move in great waves ; but
in a few moments they are down to full speed, the
head low, and the entire body stretched out to what
seems an extraordinary length. They move like
machines — flashes of fawn and mouse tints dashing
along like streaks of light, while the " Jack " bounds
away, clearing seven or eight feet at every jump, presenting to those who have never seen them under full
speed an astonishing spectacle.

The Jack almost invariably runs toward the mountains or up ; or, if there is a grove of trees near, he will
make for it, and so throw the dogs off the track. Now
he takes to a vineyard, and dogs and horses go down
the lines at the risk of their necks. The pace is killing ; the leading dog now falls back, and another surges
ahead. The Jack is beginning to realize that it is not

all pleasure, as he is losing ground. His ears, instead of being erect, are flat, and he is putting on a spurt that gives him the advance. Now he dashes into a road, and for half a mile it is a race ; the thunder of the hoofs, the cheers of the riders, raising the excitement to a high pitch. Many have dropped out, some of the dogs are winded ; but five or six are there when the Jack turns suddenly and attempts to dodge. Twice he is successful, right among the dogs and beneath the horses' feet, and then after a brief run he is seized and tossed by the leading dog. The others come up panting and distressed, while the old dog who has taken the game looks about proudly, and wags her tail in appreciation of her skill.

The lady in at the death is given the head and ears as a trophy, and, after the dogs have rested, the hunt is taken up again. One good chase will well repay the lover of such sport, that requires courage and good riding if the dogs are faithfully followed. It matters little to the true sportsman or woman how many rabbits are caught. The pleasure derived is in the very fact of being out — in the anticipation — the glorious day — the flowers, mountains, birds, horses, and dogs, and in the pleasure that the last two seem to take in it.

Instead of following the roads with which you are familiar, the hunt takes you across country where your horse beats out a wide swath in a growth of flowers which you have never heard of or seen before. You plow through them, literally a mass of color, brilliant and remarkable. Somewhere on the highlands, perhaps on the edge of the eucalyptus grove, the lunch has been carried, and here we meet a tired party of horses, dogs, and hunters. The valley stretches away before

us a coat of many colors, or a crazy quilt, in which
greens and yellows predominate; and far beyond in the
dim haze we see the ocean, thirty miles distant.

In cross country riding here, there are several things
to be considered. There are few if any fences to take,
but ditches, or rather narrow arroyos, sometimes present
themselves. A jumping horse, then, is not a necessity;
rather a fast, sure-footed one. Few horses can
keep up with greyhounds in full run; hence speed
in your mount is a *desideratum*. The horse should
be surefooted, as rabbit, owl, and badger holes or burrows are items to be thought of. In riding in a
fairly open country, these can be seen, and accidents
are rare.

Coursing is the favorite sport in Northern California,
and consists in running the dogs after rabbits, as a
simple test of speed. Around Bakersfield and various
towns in upper California, in Kern and Tulare Counties,
the Jack rabbit exists in countless numbers, and each
rancher keeps greyhounds to run them off. Occasionally
rabbit runs are indulged in; in which, by using a corral,
several thousands of the pests are caught at one time.

Among the sports in which greyhounds are used
here is coyote hunting. The coyote is the wolf of the
West, a cowardly, dog-like representative of the family,
living in the recesses of the Arroyo by night, then
coming out to arouse the dogs of the neighborhood by
its maniacal laugh or bark.

A good pack of fox-hounds or a few of these dogs
are necessary to hunt the coyotes out, and when on the
open the greyhounds soon bring them down, and a
fierce fight often ensues. A fair ground for this sport
is in the hills near Lincoln Park, or the Puente Hills,

to the south, the coyote often lurking near the sheep
which feed on the hills near here.

The sport which perhaps possesses the greatest attraction to the stranger is that of wild-cat hunting. The
wild-cat here attains a good size, weighing sometimes
fifty pounds ; hence it is well calculated to make a good
fight with the dogs. The essentials are a pack of fox-
hounds and a mount. There is little or no hard riding;
the sport consisting in seeing the skill with which the
hounds will find and tree the cats.

Mr. Arturo Bandini, of the Pasadena Hunt, owns
the finest pack in the vicinity, and to his courtesy the
lovers of sport are often indebted. The meet is generally
upon Orange Grove Avenue, or some spot contiguous
to the Arroyo. And before the dew is off the
grass, and while the scent is fresh, the musical notes
of Mr. Bandini's horn may be heard, followed by
the fitful baying of the hounds ; and then horsemen
and women come from all directions — parties from
The Raymond and other hotels, and from Los
Angeles and San Gabriel, swelling the hunt to large
proportions.

The horn brings the dogs in, and just as the sun is
coming up from Arizona the hunt winds down into the
Arroyo. The dew glistens on the leaves ; the brook,
reinforced by winter rains, rushes musically along ;
the trees — sycamores, oaks, and others — are rich in
new-born tints ; wild flowers and vines spring from
every crevice ; and one feels that, if a wild-cat is not
started, he is well repaid by seeing the green, leafy
Arroyo at early morning. The hounds are the best in
the country, and they waste no time, but soon begin
the hunt; dashing into the jungle, penetrating the

brush with noses close to the ground, uttering fitful bays, telling that they have a suspicion of game.

They cover a large area, filling the woods with, to the hunter, a melody of sounds. Then comes a short, quick series of yelps, and the dogs rush to it. Louder grows the roar, coming on the wind, making the horses dance and human pulses jump with excitement. Louder and louder it comes ; then with a rush the pack dashes by in full cry. " Stand back ! " shouts the huntsmen ; "don't cross the scent." And then the dogs having passed on, the entire field is away; some up the Arroyo, others taking the bank, scrambling among the vines and jungle ; and finally we see a dark long-tailed animal trotting along through the brush high up the bank. A red fox. It is a poor place for this sort of game, and the dogs are called back and Reynard left for the time.

Down the Arroyo the hunt goes ; some following the stream, others the road, passing beneath the bridge, and after a canter across the fields coming out above Sycamore Grove, where the cliff is high and precipitous. Here is a famous ground for cats ; and, while the horses stand beneath the great trees and girths are tightened, the dogs are taken around, and soon their musical baying comes from far above. Now it breaks into a roar, and a moment later a small gray animal breaks cover and slides down the precipice a few feet, scrambling back at the cheers that greet her. But the dogs are on the scent, and finally they work down, and dash madly through the bush. The small animal is next seen climbing or scrambling up a sycamore, and the shout of " treed " is passed along the line. A moment later and the tree is surrounded ; at its roots the pack, gazing upward with open mouths flecked with foam and eyes gleaming with excitement; back the row of horses, ladies sorry for the cat; gentlemen exultant, and all counting on the skin as a trophy.

Puss is caught, and no mistake. She sits on a limb, looking down at her tormentors with a savage gleam in her eye; her short tail twitches nervously, and is a very expressive organ. Now a small boy starts up the sycamore. As he approaches, Puss draws nearer the trunk, looks all around as if counting the chances, eyes the boy, then the dogs and cruel foes beneath. Nearer comes the boy; he taps her with a switch, and with a short run she is away fifty or sixty feet into the air — a noble jump. Down she goes; crashing into the brush, escaping the dogs by a hair's breadth, and dashing among the horses. For a moment all is confusion; then Puss is seen in another tree, and the same scene is enacted. Sometimes she escapes entirely; as a rule, the third rush is fatal, and she drops fairly into the pack; making a valiant tearing, biting, and clawing with the fury of desperation, and only succumbing to numbers.

To describe the excitement of the *finale* is difficult. The dozen or more dogs each endeavor to seize the cat, and she soon becomes a victim to their fury, consequently suffers but little. The roaring of the dogs, the snarling, the yells and shouts of the hunters, create a pandemonium hard to realize. The hounds are allowed to kill the cat; then the huntsman rushes in and endeavors to rescue it, a matter of no little difficulty; and, after a hand to hand struggle, the cat is torn away and held aloft out of their reach.

Like other sport, wild-cat hunting is fickle. Some days three or four will be caught, and again none are found.   The most propitious time is after rain, early in the morning, when the scent is fresh and before the dew and moisture have evaporated.   As a rule the hunts last from six or seven in the morning until twelve, and may be joined at any time, if the route is previously learned from the master of the hounds.

The cañons and arroyos abound in the red fox, but it is useless to hunt them, as they invariably take to the hills where horse or rider cannot follow them.   Fox hunting, however, can be had here, the country being peculiarly adapted to it.   The fox should be trapped and brought down into the open country at least five miles from the mountains.   To the lover of out-door life sport of this kind is a pleasure, in that it affords an excuse for social life in the open air.   The hunt to many is a secondary feature ; yet, if it affords entertainment and draws one from the hotel piazzas, it is to be commended.

CHAPTER XI.

MANY persons entertain the belief that Pasadena, having a dry summer, must necessarily present a burnt and verdureless appearance a portion of the year ; but never was a greater mistake. Pasadena itself is as green, indeed, in some respects more so, in sum-- mer as in winter. In the winter come the wild flowers, the hay crop, and the grains, that cover the country with rich tints of green ; while in summer we have the luxu- riant and varied foliage of the peach, apple, cherry, apricot, fig, orange, and grape in countless variety.

It may be of interest to know exactly what to expect in this ever-green land, and the following is a mere suggestion :—

Oranges, lemons, and limes are found in the market every month in the year, and may be kept a year or more on the tree. These fruits naturally ripen in February, March, or April; cherries from June to August; blackberries and apricots from June to Sep- tember. From June to January you have raspberries and peaches; from June to November, plums and prunes; nectarines, July to September; grapes from July to January; pomegranates and quinces, August to December; Japanese persimmons, November and December; loquats, April and July; guavas, all the year; currants, May and July; apples, May to February; alfalfa, five to seven crops a year; potatoes, two crops a year, and on good land two crops of grain have been

taken. By the use of a system of cold storage now
introduced here, nearly all fruits can be had at any
time during the year. Vegetables are raised all the
year round.

The large patches of green which are seen in looking down upon Pasadena from an elevation are orange
groves and vineyards. The former are ever green,
while the vineyards leaf out in early spring, and continue until the fall, as in the East, when they are all
cut back, and during the winter resemble a collection
of dead roots springing from the ground. The orange
groves, taken in masses, constitute the chief beauty of
the country. They are always green, and the blossom,
bud, ripe and green fruit, may be seen upon the tree
at the same time.

The orange was probably introduced into this country from Spain ; and the oldest trees, seventy years
or more, are to be found down at San Gabriel. Hardly
a portion of Pasadena but boasts a grove ; in fact, the
city is laid out in a vast orange grove. Orange Grove
Avenue, the finest resident street, is cut through one.
Many of these have been neglected or lawns allowed
to grow up around them, so they do not produce as fine
fruit as may be found elsewhere.

Examples of extensive groves may be seen at Baldwin's and Rose's ranches. At Kinneyloa many different
varieties are seen, as the seedling, Mediterranean sweet,
the Washington Navel, the blood orange, mandarin, and
many more. The Navel is seedless, and took the prize
over all oranges of this country at the New Orleans
Exposition.

The orange groves of Pasadena range from one or
two up to fifteen years old. Trees will bear when three

or four years old, and begin to pay when five or six. What has been done, and what one can do with an orange grove, are two very different things. Many people in Pasadena obtain a fair living from their groves, while others do not.

ORANGE PICKING.

The grove of Col. B. D. Wilson has been known to yield $1,800 per acre per season, each tree producing oranges valued at $70. The following statement is quoted to show the possibilities; but it will be noticed

that in the immediate vicinity of the crown of the valley
land cannot be obtained at the price quoted.

OUTLAY.

Ten acres of land . . .	$1,000
One thousand trees	750
Planting and caring for same first season at $25 per acre	250
Caring for orchard second year at $15 per acre	150
Third year $15 per acre .	150
Fourth year $20 per acre .	200
Fifth year $25 per acre .	250
Extras	550
Total .	$3,300
Interest on investment . .	1,000
Total	$4,300

RECEIPTS.

Third year a few oranges for home consumption.
Fourth year, 50 oranges to the tree; 50,000 at $20
per 100, $1,000. Fifth year, 200 to the tree; 200,000
oranges at $20 per 100, $4,000. This estimate is based
on the books of a Pasadenian in 1885. Since then
there have been many changes; chief of which is the
advance in land. There are in Southern California
over half a million bearing orange trees. This means
in the past season a shipment of 2,500 car loads East.
A car contains about 300 boxes, which gives us 750,000
oranges — California's winter offering to the East.

The trees attain nearly their full development at fifteen years, and may then be twenty-three or twenty-
four feet high, with a trunk three feet in circumference.
Such a tree may bear four thousand oranges a season;

the retail value of which in the East would be
$200.

The orange, lemon, and lime trees are the ones which
need irrigation, being watered well three or four times
during the season. This is done by scooping up
basins about the trees, and connecting them by canals,
so that the basins are all filled.

The sight of a grove laden with the golden fruit is a
very attractive one. Later, the Indian, Mexican, and
American gangs of pickers go around, and pyramids of
the golden spheres are seen in the groves. The fruit
is washed, wiped, and sorted according to size and color,
and finally shipped, to compete with the Mediterranean
and Florida productions. On many ranches, as Rose's
and Baldwin's, and near the old mill are fine groves of
the English walnut. The trees are extremely beautiful,
and those of some orchards realize $200 per acre in
the season. The tree comes into bearing when about
ten years old. Some fine examples may be seen on
Walnut Street.

The vast vineyards that cover miles of country here
attract attention in the winter by their grotesque
appearance, resembling roots set on end with some
regularity. This is due to the fact that every fall the
vines are cut back. All summer they are at their
best, and in the autumn loaded with grapes, the
bunches of the mission variety often weighing over
five pounds. Most of the vintage here goes to the
great wineries of Shorb, Baldwin, or Rose, and in
other localities are made into raisins. In 1885
Southern California sent out over half a million boxes,
and proposes in time to rule the business. In 1884
fifty-three million pounds of raisins were sent into this

country from Europe, with high tariff.   In the future
California can meet this entire demand.   The present
volume is merely intended to suggest interesting features to the tourist ; and in the various industries of

A PASADENA VINEYARD.

the San Gabriel one may find an extended field.
California can supply the entire country with wine,
preserved fruit, olives, nuts, small fruits, raisins,
oranges, lemons, limes, and many of the articles now

imported.   At Linda Vista the visitor will find an
experimental station, where forest trees are to be
planted.   The Hon.   Abbot Kinney, of Lamanda
Park, is the Commissioner of Forestry in this section.
In almost every place in the city are found fig trees,
bearing a large crop of this valuable fruit, and some
large groves have been established.   The fact that
we import nearly eight million pounds of figs yearly
is suggestive of the possibilities in this direction.

So with the olive.   The northeastern portion of
Pasadena is called Olivewood, as here was originally
planted a large olive grove; and on the slopes near
Millard Cañon an olive grove was started some years
ago that would have been the largest in the world,
had not the land increased so in value that the idea
was abandoned.   In San Diego County olive trees are
known to pay $100 to $150 per tree.   There are up
to date about a thousand acres in California planted
with olives.   Good-sized trees may be seen upon any
of the large ranches.

The tourist will notice in the Pasadena landscape
square blocks of forest trees rising plume-like to a
height of from sixty to one hundred feet.   These are
eucalyptus forests or groves, planted for fire wood by
ranchers who have land to spare.   Taking an actual
case, a rancher planted sixty acres with twenty-six
thousand eucalyptus plants which cost $10 a thousand.
Planting, plowing, and cultivating, including the hire
of a man for six months, cost, including the trees,
nearly $1,000, which was the expense for the first year.
The second year it cost $480, after which there was
no expense.   The trees grow rapidly, and at five
years are large enough to cut.

SANTA ANITA CLUB-HOUSE AND LAKE.

CHAPTER XII.

Poppies, Yucca, Cacti, Trees, etc.

FLORIDA has been called the land of flowers, but it was because the floral possibilities of Southern California were unknown. Between the two there is no comparison. As winter approaches in the land of gold, form after form appears, until in mid-winter the wealth of verdure is bewildering to the eye.

The *mesas*, that have been burnt and brown, at the bidding of the first rain assume a change of raiment — first green, with the rapid growing *alfileria*, so valuable as natural fodder. This covers the length and breadth of the land, marking the high and by ways with new-born tints, while the little star-shaped pink blossom lends loveliness by the contrast. Soon after the advent of the *alfileria* comes a delicate, bell-shaped, cream-colored flower, daintily poised aloft on slender stalk. On the upper slopes they mass like snow, changing the color of the fields. In February, or possibly earlier, comes the poppy. Splashes of color appear here and there; the afterglow of the mountains seems to have been transferred to the plains below, and finally the slopes appear afire with the golden flower. In certain places — near cañons, on the hills of San Rafael ranch, and in Wilson's Cañon — the "shooting star," or American cowslip, is found. Yellow violets now appear, covering the ground in

PROPOSED UNION CLUB BUILDING, COLORADO STREET.

many places, nodding in clumps in the grain fields, or forming a gorgeous border to the roadside, together with masses of a little blue cup-shaped flower — the "baby bluetts" of the children.   At first we may keep the newcomers well in hand; but now others follow so quickly that we are lost in confusion.   The painter's brush colors the hillsides and fields with vivid tints, resting on a matting of velvet greens, formed by clovers of many kinds.   The iris rears its graceful shape in brilliant masses, while evening primrose, rock rose, wild pea, tulip, and many more are distinguishable in the floral throng.   Bells of blue and white, trumpets of purple and pink, the lovely *Penstemon*, the gorgeous silene, huge ox-eyed daisies, delicate crucifers, golden dandelions, blue and white snapdragons, pale pink morning glories, and count-less others make up this winter greeting, which can-not be described or even enumerated here.   The lilies are of especial beauty.   A curious lavender one, the Mariposa lily, is found late in the season at Lincoln Park, near the fields of wild mustard, that bears gold dust on its stalks.   Washington's lily, Parry's, and Humboldt's are all here, while the treas-ured calla of the East is an alien hedge plant.

The common plant of the *mesa* is the sage, among which flourishes the *yerba santa* of the Mexicans, a local "cure all."   The slopes of the mountains are covered with rich flowering shrubs.   Here is the scarlet gooseberry (*Ribis speciosum*), with its barberry-like flower.   This has been introduced into Pasadena by Mrs. Jeanne C. Carr, the well-known and distin-guished botanist; her beautiful home, on the corner of Colorado Street and Orange Grove Avenue, affording

OUT-DOOR LIFE AT PASADENA IN JANUARY.

examples. The plant can be seen growing wild on the Scoville trail, back of the city. The cacti attract the attention of the tourist, and many different kinds can be found in the Arroyo and *mesa*.

One of the most striking plants is the yucca (*Yucca Baccata*). Two species are seen in the Arroyo and on the foot-hills, sending up a stalk upon which hang innumerable white bells that jangle in the soft wind — music that reaches man as incense. At a distance these bells form a gleaming mass of white, and, standing amid the bayonet leaves, vividly call to mind a candle-stick; and so it has been called "The Candle-stick of the Lord."

The forest trees are principally in the cañons and upon the lofty northern slopes of the Sierras : Douglas firs, Coulter pines, fine large oaks ; the black variety of the plain often having a spread of one hundred and fifty feet. In former years the live oaks were extremely common about Pasadena, and some fine specimens still stand in the Wilson pasture.

In the arroyos and cañons the sycamore is the most conspicuous, and near the Devil's Gate are some fine trees. The cotton wood is also a familiar form, and in the upper cañons the bay tree lends fragrance to the air. The possibilities of forestry in Southern California can best be appreciated and understood after a visit to "Carmelita," the home of Mrs. Carr, where almost every tree in this country, and many from foreign lands, may be seen.

To the lover of flowers or botany in the abstract, this region offers a most interesting study, from the ferns and giant brakes of the cañons to the lofty firs of the upper Sierras.

CHAPTER XIII.

Santa Monica, Long Beach, Santa Catalina, San Pedro, etc.

A REFERENCE to Pasadena would be incomplete without mention of its resources in the way of seaside resorts. In previous chapters the cañons, mountains, valleys, arroyos, and other inland retreats have been referred to as of especial interest to the invalid who may desire a change. Pasadena is equally rich in resorts at the sea level, and in little more than an hour one may descend from the nine hundred feet which constitute its altitude, and enjoy, winter or summer, the pleasures of ocean bathing.

Santa Monica is the natural watering-place of the county, and destined to be the most important in the future. The summer climate is always cool, while the winter is milder if anything than that of the interior, and the change between day and night somewhat less. The town, which stands upon a high bluff over one hundred feet above the ocean, in a commanding position, is composed of comfortable and attractive homes, embowered with a profusion of tropical plants and trees. Here are numerous hotels, a fine beach for bathing, and a condition of things in winter extremely peculiar to the tourist from the East.

Santa Monica in winter is surrounded by a rich green sward, spreading away for miles, and to the north reaching up to the Sierra Santa Monica range of mountains, that abound in beautiful, well-wooded cañons, inhabited only by the bee-keepers. In this proximity to the mountains Santa Monica combines the pleasures of inland and seaside; and one may ride along the beach, and turn up one of the little cañons, and find him or herself in a few moments apparently far from every suggestion of the ocean.

Santa Monica is the fashionable watering-place of Southern California. Here is the Casino, built after the plan of the one at Newport. The lawn tennis tournaments are held here and the fashionable balls of the season. The beach affords a horseback ride of twenty miles or more. To the north the mountains reach down to the water, and here the sea has broken through and formed an arch of interesting appearance. Santa Monica can be reached from Pasadena by cars in little over an hour; but in winter, when the rains have laid the dust, it is a delightful trip either on horseback or by carriage, the road leading by old ranches and through fields of flowers, skirting the Sierra Santa Monica range.

Long Beach is the next watering-place, ranked according to distance. It can be reached by rail in less than two hours, while good carriage roads lead to it. The beach here is finer than at Santa Monica, allowing driving at any time. Good hotels and cottages have been built, and a thriving and attractive seaside town is the result, calling to mind Asbury Park, on the New Jersey coast.

Between Santa Monica and Long Beach lie San Pedro and Wilmington, the former interesting as being the port of entry of Los Angeles. Here the yachts of

the Los Angeles Club make their headquarters, and
the steamer starts for one of the most interesting
localities in the vicinity — Santa Catalina Island.

The island is about thirty miles off shore, seventeen
miles long, and from five to seven miles wide.   It
is a mountain range — a disconnected spur of the
Sierra Madres — rising up through the blue waters of
the Pacific.   The only available level land is in the
cañons, or where they open out and reach the ocean.
The largest of these, at the southeastern end of the
island, has been selected as a hotel site, a wharf
built, and here hundreds of tenters make their
summer home.   The upper range is easily gained
on horseback, and extended rides may be taken
over the entire island.   On reaching the west side,
the scene is grand and impressive.   You sit upon
your horse, and look over the edge of an almost
sheer precipice that falls away for fifteen hundred or
two thousand feet.   The waves are seen breaking
upon the rocks far below — so far that the sound does
not reach you.   The bark of the sea lion comes
faintly from the rocks off shore; and the bits of fog
blowing in, partly intercepting the view, give an idea
of greater height above the ocean.   Years ago the
island was stocked with goats that are now fairly wild,
and afford some sport to the hunter who enjoys hard
riding and climbing.   The charm of Catalina lies in
its rocky shores, its miniature bays, differing from the
shore of the mainland.   The fishing is good in season;
and the temperature here, like that of Coronado
Beach, varies but little day after day, while the nights
are much more mild than localities on the mainland.
A summer at Catalina may be compared to an ocean
voyage — without the discomforts.

The hotel at Catalina is built upon the site of an old Indian graveyard, and numbers of interesting relics of bygone days have been unearthed.   Two hundred years ago the island sustained a large native population ; but time and causes about which little or nothing is known have tended to produce their utter extinction.

In the future, probably many of the bays or cañon openings will be built up with towns or villages. Santa Barbara is within a few hours of Pasadena, and San Diego and Coronado Beach, four hours — facts which point to its being the centre of all the principal points of interest.

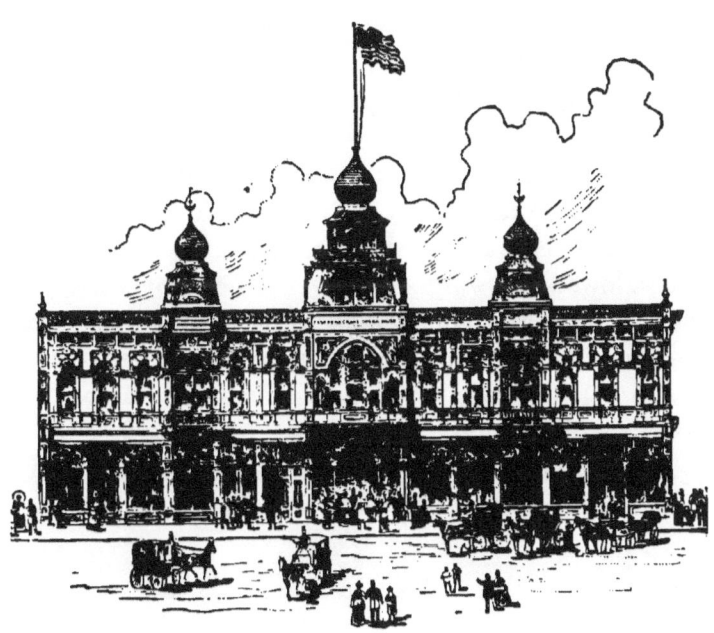

GRAND OPERA HOUSE, RAYMOND AVENUE.

CHAPTER XIV.

The Indian village of Pachanga. Camulos. San Fernando Mission.
San Juan, etc.

PASADENA is the centre of a most interesting region midway between Santa Barbara, San Diego, and other localities famous for their historical reminiscences.

From Pasadena in any direction excellent roads lead away; and for hundreds of miles one can travel on highways quite as good as those in the cities and towns, with the assurance of finding good accommodations at short intervals.

This makes long rides, not only possible, but delightful; and the object of the present chapter is to point out some which are especially desirable. For a drive of three or four days or a week, a party may be made up of four, six, or more people. A good double team is required, with seats according to the number, and a saddle horse may be taken to be used in turn by gentlemen or ladies, and for the latter a side-saddle can be conveniently fastened to the axle and allowed to swing. A driver is not a necessity, as there is little or no chance of losing the way. A good plan is to take a lunch each day, to be enjoyed picnic fashion on the road wherever one may be, taking the other meals at hotels.

Trip number one may be to the Pala Mission, in San Diego County. Leaving Pasadena early in the morning, we drive through San Gabriel, skirt Puente and the low country thereabouts, following the mountains, that are five or six miles away, wind among the hills, passing many old Mexican adobes, reaching Pomona by three or four o'clock. After passing the night at the Hotel Palomares, in early morning we drive around town and away to the east through an uninteresting country — almost a desert, were it not for the flowers. Ontario is in sight a few miles distant, and we make the Ontario Hotel for dinner, take a ride on the grand fifteen-mile drive that leads up to the mountains, and are off for the east again, twenty miles or so, to San Bernadino.

Here the country is flat and uninteresting, covered with low bush, and the road at times sandy, though when passed over by the writer in fair shape. To the south the railroad is seen, and the curious volcano-like peaks about Riverside. Near the range are several ranches of interest, as that of Mr. Petch, where trees of all kinds may be seen in a high state of cultivation, showing what can be done with water in what appears a desert.

San Bernadino is reached at night; and, if the Arrow Head Springs are to be visited, the party would stay here; if not, another hour will take them through Colton, and so on to Riverside to The Glenwood, which is cozy and homelike. From Riverside the road to Perris is taken, passing Elsinore and its famous lake, Lucerne, with its coal mines, terra cotta, etc., reaching Murrietta at night. From here a visit should be made to the Santa Rosa ranch, owned by Parker Dear, Esq., which occupies seventy-two square miles on the crest of the Temecula range. A day can

be well spent here and in the lovely cañons of the
range.

From here we pass the old ranches of Murrietta and
Gonzales, the latter the site of an ancient village. The
writer is indebted to Mr. Gonzales for many interesting relics found here. Down through the barren town
of Temecula we drive, and are now in the country
described by " H. H. " in " Ramona." Over to the left,
up a little valley, is the ranch of Mrs. Ramona Wolf,
where Mrs. Jackson obtained much valuable material
for her literary work. Near by is the now deserted
graveyard where Ramona waited while Alessandro
went to the half store, half inn, to pawn his violin.
The country about possesses a peculiar charm. There
are old memories at every mile post.

Here is Judge Magee's, where we may pick up an
Indian to guide us; for not far away is the old
village of Pachanga, where the Indian is seen living
in his picturesque hut perched on hill tops, with leafy
ramada about it. Here the *matate* is still used, and
huge stone mortars lie about. The younger genera-
tion speak a guttural Mexican patois, but the old men
and women use the Indian tongue. Here Indian
baskets can be bought, about which there is such a
craze. The small ones are worth from 50 cents
to $1.50 for bowls and plaques, while the large fruit
baskets bring from $2 to $4.

Pachanga is well worth a visit; and, if the long
carriage ride is not desired, the Santa Fè road can be
taken to Murrietta and carriages hired here.

Leaving Pachanga we continue over fine roads, leaving the Santa Fè road as it cuts through the mountains,
and head for Palomar, or Smith's Mountain. The

road now leads through a magnificent cañon, rocky, and abounding in grand scenery. For two hours we wind down, passing several adobe ruins and flourishing ranches, and finally come out in the attractive Pala Valley at the old Mission of that name, where we shall receive a warm welcome from Mrs. Veal, a sister of Mrs. Wolf, whose husband keeps the only hotel, an adobe house, at which " H. H." stopped during her tour in this section. The railroad has not reached Pala yet, and it is a quiet, attractive spot, well worthy the trip. From here we may in a day visit the Pauma Mission, about ten miles up the valley; but it hardly repays the ride, though the Indian village there will perhaps produce some baskets. This trip will, if followed leisurely, take a week. The return may be made to the west of the range, or back by Riverside, down Santa Ana Cañon, and back through Orange, Fulton Wells, etc.

An interesting ride from Pasadena is to the Mission of San Juan Capistrano. This occupies two or three days. The road takes us through San Gabriel, skirting Whittier, Santa Fè Springs, Anaheim, Santa Ana, Tustin, and Orange; San Juan being about twenty-two miles from the latter and about three miles from the Pacific. The old Mission, founded in 1776, though fast going to decay, still shows signs of ancient splendor. The country hereabouts is attractive, especially in winter; groves of cotton-wood and eucalypti lending beauty to the situation. San-Juan-by-the-Sea is the next place west, and from here the road can be followed leading down to San Diego, passing the thriving seaside resorts of Del Mar, Carlsbad, Ocean Side, etc.; but for a carriage ride San Juan Capistrano is the best terminus. The Santa Fè road now passes through this region. Here is the famous Laguna ranch and the rich ranches of the Santa Ana Valley.

A third ride, occupying two days, is to the San Fernando Rey Mission. The road up the La Cañada Valley can be taken, or by passing through Glendale and following the railroad. This Mission was established in 1797. There is a good hotel at San Fernando or in its immediate vicinity.

The San Fernando Rey Mission is in the centre of the township of that name, and was built by moneys provided by Charles IV., of Spain, and the Marquis of Branceforte, Viceroy of Mexico. It was erected in honor of Ferdinande V., King of Castile and Aragon.

Like the other missions it is falling to decay; but in the good old times, with its out-buildings, it extended for nearly a mile and a half. The greater number of missions have entirely disappeared, while others are represented by mounds of disintegrating adobe earth.

The olive trees about the old Mission were planted by the Franciscan Fathers before the adoption of the Constitution of the United States. The ancient trees still produce an abundant supply of fruit.

The Camulos ranch will be remembered as the home of Ramona, and is one of the few old places remaining in Ventura County. Here the old customs are still kept up, and in July of every year the annual *fiesta* of the Dal Valle family is held. Camulos is a long day's drive northwest of Pasadena, perhaps forty-five or fifty miles. Mrs. Jackson was at Camulos only a few hours, yet she has given a vivid description of the home in "Ramona," and the visitor

should read the book before making the trip. Mr.
Charles F. Lummis, city editor of the *Los Angeles
Times*, has published a handbook of Camulos, giving
photographs of the points of interest referred to in
"Ramona," which will add to the interest of the visit.
The *fiesta* is a gathering of the family and their friends
at the old homestead. It generally lasts for four
days, during which time the guests of Camulos number
from seventy-five to one hundred ladies and gentlemen. Each day is given over to some different
pleasure. An entire ox is killed and eaten, the old
dances are revived, and fair women and gallant gentlemen toast the old memories.

Santa Barbara can be easily made by carriage.
Indeed, this method of traveling is a very common one
in Southern California, and many tourists with their
own teams travel from Pasadena to San Francisco and
beyond in this way.

In the summer the range of the Sierra Madres is
frequented by campers, who penetrate the deep cañons
and enjoy the pure air of the upper range. San
Antonio Cañon is within a day's drive of Pasadena,
and here one may find scenery of the most varied
description. Camp may be formed up the cañon by
the side of the trout stream, and the trip made to the
summit of Old Baldy, or Mount San Antonio, as it
should be called. From here, where one can possibly
snowball in July, the most remarkable view on the
American continent is to be had. Away to the east
stretches the desert of Arizona, a tract so barren and
deadly that few have ever attempted it in midsummer;
while to the west, separated by the mountains, lies the
most fertile country in the world, glowing with fruit

and flower.   On one hand rise the lofty rain clouds of
the Arizona wet season; on the other it is summer,
and no rain falls.   So strange a condition of affairs
climatic can be seen no where else in this country.

PROPOSED YOUNG MEN'S CHRISTIAN ASSOCIATION BUILDING.

CHAPTER XV.

THE FAUNA.

Spiders, Lizards, Snakes, Natural curiosities, Trap-door Spiders, Birds, etc.

WHILE Pasadena has an interesting fauna, it is absolutely free from any insects or other animals dangerous in any way. The rattlesnake is found in Southern California, the tarantula, centipede, and scorpion; but one might live in Pasadena ten years, and never know that they were included in the fauna. The writer has ridden through the brush and over every portion of the outlying country for three years, and has seen but one rattlesnake. Around the city they are never found, and in the outlying country they are rarely if ever seen. So that one may feel perfect security — at least the same one would feel in the East — in making excursions to the cañons and various haunts of interest. The objectionable insects have to be hunted for. The scorpions here are sub-terranean in their habits, living under stones and in the ground, and rarely are seen. The big tarantula has a similar habit, living in a deep burrow with an open mouth, generally covered over with a web. These monsters have a spread of four or five and even more inches, but are cowardly, having to be dug out or tempted by running a stick into the burrow. It is the generally accepted and popular belief that it is the big tarantula that makes the trap-doors; but this is an error. The big spider is known as *Tarantula Henzei*, and simply makes a burrow. The trap-door maker is a smaller spider, known scientifically as *Cteniza California*. The trap-doors, which are familiar objects in all the shops, are the ingenious work of these little creatures. A long tunnel is built, lined with silk, and a door of silk and adobe formed, adjusted so perfectly that it is water-tight and self-closing. The tops of the Puente Hills, back of The Raymond, afford numberless examples of these little homes, while the larger spiders can be found in the fields out of the city. A shovel or pick is a requisite in the hunt.

The winter at Pasadena is sufficiently cool to force the snakes into a state of coma known as a winter sleep, and one of these reptiles is rarely if ever seen from November to April. During this season they are coiled up beneath the ground in burrows or holes. A variety of beautiful lizards are seen, but the chill of winter nights sends them into a partial state of hibernation, though the warm midday sun often brings them out again. One of the most attractive of these little creatures has a rich mottled brown body, with a tail of vivid blue. It is rarely seen, and then only for a moment. When the flowers appear, a variety of attractive butterflies come out; and a lumbering black beetle, popularly known as the bombardier, is a common sight. Touch him, and he raises his canon-like body upon his long legs, and discharges from two little glands a yellowish liquid, poisonous to many animals and extremely disagreeable to a human enemy. It is the defence of the beetle, and a most effective one.

Among the mammals not previously referred to, are badgers, large, flat fellows, the makers of many of the big burrows found on the *mesa;* ground squirrels, which, with the wood rats, give rise to the popular saying that in California the rats live in trees and the squirrels in the ground. The squirrels are seen everywhere in vacant lots, sharing the upper crust with the gopher (*Geomys*), that forms tunnels much after the fashion of the mole, though doing far more damage.

The wood rat (*neotama*) bears some resemblance to the common rat, though having a shorter tail. The big bunches of grass and other material sometimes seen in trees, and again about the roots of small trees, are their homes.

There is also a jumping rat, " pocket rat," kangaroo rat (*Dipodomys*), passing under many names, an attractive little creature, with long hind legs like those of a kangaroo. It is crepuscular in its habits, and rarely seen. On each side of the mouth are pockets, in which large numbers of seeds can be stowed away.

Two species of skunks are found here, a large and a small. They are rarely seen or met with, though the small ones, beautiful animals, have a curious habit of taking up their abode in the walls of houses when they can obtain entrance. They soon drive out rats and mice, and, when the offensive glands have been removed, they make interesting pets.

The loon is very abundant in the arroyos ; and on the *mesas* a reddish-brown little animal, the weasel, is sometimes seen. In the upper range a wolf is occasionally shot; and the coyote and fox represent it lower down. The eastern toad is missed here. In place of it there is a heavy, clumsy toad, seemingly a link between a toad and a frog; it comes out at night from beneath the brush. A small toad, something like a tree toad, is found upon the rocks of the cañons, mimicking them in color to a remarkable extent; and by the lake on San Rafael ranch the same little creature is often found upon the leaves of water-loving plants.

In the winter time myriads of birds are found in the valley. Here they winter or stay awhile on their voyage to the extreme south. They range in size from the huge condor, having a stretch of wing nine feet across, to the delicate humming-bird.

The robin here is not the joyous bird of the East, in tone and color being more subdued. The meadow lark is the glorious tuner, and in the season its notes are heard the length and breadth of the land.

Here are several thrushes, one with a curved bill and remarkable song or note. Butcher birds haunt every grove, impaling lizards and insects upon the thorns. The turtle dove is more than common, its mournful note ringing in every eucalyptus grove; and in the upper cañon is found the mountain pigeon, a magnificent bird weighing two or three pounds.

Owls we have in great numbers, from a great horned variety, found in lonesome cañons, to the "monkey face" and little burrower of the lowlands. Orioles, warblers, mocking birds, woodpeckers, crow blackbirds, and a host of others are here, but the woodcock and Eastern quail are absent.

A characteristic bird is the chaparral cock or road runner or *paisano*, that runs along the byways with marvelous speed. Its eye is a marvel of beauty, not to say ferocity. It is of this bird that the rattlesnake corral story is told; the bird, it is said, building a corral of cactus leaves about the rattler, then awakening him to destruction on the spines. This story is generally considered a "fable;" though I have been told the story by men who had watched the bird build the corral, and a well-known surveyor in this county states that he has found the corrals, with the skeleton of the snake in the centre. There is possibly some mistake in the observations, though the story is not more wonderful than that of the gardener bird, and many more known to be true. In fall and spring the lakes abound in water birds; a fine plover is often seen well inland, and a variety of shore birds. The Jack snipe is sometimes shot about Pasadena, though more common at the Chino ranch, over by Pomona.

A variety of cranes and herons accompany the army of emigrants, and occasionally a brown pelican is seen. Of ducks and geese there is a surfeit; the *honk honk* of the wild goose being often heard, while flocks of thousands are seen following the Sierras by night and day — north or south, as the case may be. To the lover of nature the fauna here is of great interest, and affords a wide field for the investigator.

HINTS TO TOURISTS.

The climate of Pasadena is so mild in winter, allowing the blooming of flowers throughout the season, that the impression is sometimes conveyed that this is a tropical climate, and many persons come prepared for a Cuban season. In matters of dress no change should be made from the East. In fact, Southern Californians dress, season for season, as Bostonians or New Yorkers do. In the winter months an overcoat is always needed at night, and sometimes in early morning and later in the day.   In summer ordinary Eastern summer clothing is required.

After exercising violently at tennis or riding, a newcomer should stand in the sun to get cool, instead of seeking a shade tree, as in the East.   The difference between the sunlight and shade here makes this an important feature to a delicate person.   After acclimatization it is not noticed.

TABLE OF COMPARATIVE CLIMATES.

Place	Approximate Elevation	Monthly Mean for January	Monthly Mean for July	Number of Years Observed	Difference between Jan. and July	Annual Mean	Rainfall
San Francisco	20	51	58	10	7	55	23.96
Sacramento	32	46	73	4	27	60	25.94
Visalia	326	40	90	3	34	62	10.46
El Paso, Tex	3550	52	79	1	39	60	10.50
City of Mexico	7469	71	65		13	60	10.50
Honolulu		68	78		7	75	
Auckland		67	49		19	58	
Melbourne		62	43		18	59	
Sidney, N. S. W.		63	54		8	62	
Ceylon Hills		69	71		2	70	
Canton, China		52	83		31	69	
Nagasaki, Jap.		43	80		37		
Jerusalem		47	77		30	62	
Cairo, Egypt		58	85		27	72	
Malta Island		56	78		22	67	
Madeira Island		59	69		10	65	
Cadiz, Spain		51	70		19	63	
Marseilles, Fr.		43	73		32	59	
Bordeaux		41	73		32		
Paris		35	64		29		
Nice		45	75		30	51	
Mentone, Italy		40	74		33	59	
Milan		33	74		41	60	
Florence		41	72		33	61	
Rome		47	76		25		
Naples		46	72		30		
London		37	62		25		

Place	Approximate Elevation	Monthly Mean for January	Monthly Mean for July	Number of Years Observed	Difference between Jan. and July	Annual Mean	Rainfall
Pasadena	900	52	67	6	15	61.75	19
Los Angeles	293	52	67	6	15	60	12.88
San Bernadino	1800	51	70		19		.23
Santa Barbara	*	52	62	7	15	60	15
San Diego	48	53	66	9	13		10.01
Fort Yuma	140	52	89	1	37		2.30
St. Marks, Fla.	15	52	81	5	27	68	61.30
Pensacola, Fla.	30	54	81	2	28	69	55.94
Jacksonville	43	55	83	8	32	68	34.74
San Antonio	657	52	84	2	28	69	65.93
New Orleans	10	54	82		46	49	14.77
Denver, Col.	5250	26	72	10	57	43	29.59
St. Paul, Minn.	779	15	72	10	33	62	36.50
Atlanta, Ga.	1054	46	71	3	40	50	50.20
Newport, R. I.	30	31	71	6	44	48	49.47
Boston, Mass.	15	27	71	10	45	46	37.30
Buffalo, N. Y.	589	26	74	10	44	51	42.70
New York City	50	30	76	10	45	53	41.89
Philadelphia	50	31	79	10	44	55	42.40
Baltimore	12	34	79	10	44	55	42.34
Washington	37	35	79	10	48	55	43.75
Cincinnati	553	34	78	10	48	49	43.63
Chicago	592	25	73	10	55	55	35.47
St. Louis	464	31	79	10	53	49	39.10
Omaha	1054	21	76	9	44	52	33.05
Leavenworth	808	26	79	7	53	51	31.30
Salt Lake City	4295	29	77	8	44	53	17.52
Portland, Or.	50	39	67		28		53.26

* Sea level.

RELATIVE HUMIDITY.

Name of Place.	Relative Humidity.		
	For the warmest six months.	For the coolest six months.	For the year.
Pasadena........................	67	56	56
Los Angeles, California	66	64	65
San Diego, California	75	69	72
Santa Barbara, California	71	67	69
Visalia, California	42	72	57
San Francisco, California..........	74	72	73
Portland, Oregon	66	77	71
Denver, Colorado	41	50	45
Santa Fé, New Mexico.........	35	46	41
St. Paul, Minnesota	66	70	68
Chicago, Illinois	69	71	70
New York City....................	66	68	67
Boston, Massachusetts	69	70	70
Ashville, North California.........	79	65	72
Jacksonville, Florida.............	70	69	70
New Orleans, Louisiana	69	70	70

POINTS OF INTEREST AND DISTANCES FROM PASADENA.

Switzer's Camp . . . . 13 miles.

Baldwin's Ranch, Race Course, etc. . . 5 miles.

Rose's Winery, Ranch, etc. . . . . . . 4 miles.

San Gabriel Mission · . . . . 2½ miles.

Old Mill (El Molino) . . . . 2 miles.

Stoneman's Ranch . . . . 1 mile.

San Rafael Ranch . . . . ½ mile.

Las Cacitas . . . . 4 miles.

Negro Cañon . . . . 4 miles.

Wilson's Peak . . . . 8 miles.

Eaton's Cañon	5 miles.
Las Flores Cañon	4 miles.
Millard Cañon	4 miles.
Arroyo Seco Cañon	4 miles.
Verdugo Cañons	7 miles.
Ostrich Farm	1½ miles.
Sierra Madre Villa	6 miles.
Mount Disappointment	15 miles.
Brown's Peak	8 miles.
Wilson's Cañon	2 miles.
Linda Vista	2 miles.
Linda Vista Trail	1¾ miles.
Fremont Trail	½ mile.
Eagle Rock	1 mile.
Giddings' Trail	4 miles.
Las Cacitas Trail	4 miles.
Devil's Gate	2½ miles.
Devil's Gate Park	2 miles.
Monk Hill	2 miles.
Oak Knoll	1 mile.
San Gabriel Winery	3 miles.
Puente Hills	4 miles.
Los Angeles	9 miles.
Garvanza	3 miles.
Eagle Rock Valley	3 miles.
La Cañada Valley	4½ miles.
Altadena	3 miles.
Sierra Madre Mountains	4 miles.
San Rafael Hills	½ mile.
Olivewood	1 mile.
San Rafael Tunnel	1 mile.
Lincoln Park	2 miles.
Arroyo Park	3 miles.

CHURCHES AND SOCIETIES OF PASADENA.

SOCIETIES.

SELECT KNIGHTS A. O. U. W.— Pasadena Legion
No. 18. G. M. Boston, Commander; J. Mills, Recorder. At Library Hall, every Tuesday evening.

Pasadena Lodge No. 151. Thursday evenings in
Library Hall. L. C. Winston, M. W.; Theo. Coleman,
Recorder.

I. O. O. F.— Pasadena Lodge No. 324. Wednesday evenings, at Odd Fellows' Hall. S. P. Swear-
ingen, M. D., N. G.; G. F. Peabody, R. S.

Pasadena Encampment No. 84. Second and fourth
Friday evenings at Odd Fellows' Hall, Doty Block.
W. H. Darrow, C. P.; A. C. Stevens, H. P.; W. Blick,
Scribe.

Rebecca Degree Lodge No. 121, I. O. O. F. Meets
in Odd Fellows' Hall first and third Monday evenings
of each month at 7.30. V. Martin, N. G.; H. C.
Mohn, Secretary.

K. OF L.— Pasadena Assembly No. 1051. Meets in
Library Hall the second and fourth Saturday evenings
of each month at 7.30. F. W. Bunnell, Secretary.

G. A. R.— John F. Godfrey Post No. 93. Second
and fourth Tuesday evenings of each month in Library
Hall. Visiting comrades cordially invited. W. B.
Vankirk, P. C.; A. C. Drake, Adjutant.

WOMAN'S RELIEF CORPS.— Meets the second and
fourth Monday afternoon of each month in Library
Hall, at 2.30. Visiting sisters cordially invited. President, Mrs. C. B. Clapp; Secretary, Mrs. Virginia
Rippey.

SONS OF VETERANS.— Phil Kearny Camp No. 7.
Meets at Library Hall every Monday evening at 7.30.

Jas. Campbell, Capt. Comdg.; S. L. Wallis, 1st Sergeant.

K. of P. — Pasadena Lodge No. 132. Every Tuesday, at Odd Fellows' Hall. Visiting knights always welcome. C. H. Stratton, C. C.; G. F. Peabody, K. of R. and S.

I. O. G. T. — Pasadena Lodge No. 173. Friday evening, Library Hall. Chas. B. Gray, W. C. T.; H. M. Cole, W. S.

BROTHERHOOD OF CARPENTERS AND JOINERS OF PASADENA, Union No. 195. — Meetings every Monday, at 7.30 P. M., at Mills' Hall. Visiting brothers cordially invited.

F. & A. M. — Pasadena Lodge No. 272. Stated meetings fourth Monday of each month, in Masonic Hall. Visiting brethren cordially invited. R. Williams, Master; W. S. Nosworthy, Secretary.

W. C. T. U. — The ladies of this society meet at the Baptist Church on the first Thursday and the third Thursday of each month, at 3.00 P. M. Cordial invitation to all, whether members or not.

PASADENA ACADEMY OF SCIENCES. — Meet the second Tuesday in each month, subject to previous call. Hon. Delos Arnold, President; W. L. Vail, Recording Secretary.

PUBLIC LIBRARY.

Open daily from 9.00 A. M. to 9.30 P. M. Reading-room free, and 25 cents per month for taking books. Mrs. S. E. Merritt, Librarian.

CITY OFFICERS.

Trustees. — M. M. Parker, Chairman of the Board;

J. B. Young, A. G. Throop, Edson Turner, S. Townsend.

Clerk and Assessor, Jas. H. Cambell; Treasurer, Col. J. Banbury; Tax Collector and Chief of Police, I. N. Mundell.

Board of Education. — Z. Decker, R. Williams, C. W. Buchanan.

CHURCHES.

MONK HILL CONGREGATIONAL.— Sunday school and gospel service, Fair Oaks Avenue, opposite Painter Hotel. Services every Sunday at 2.30 P. M. Rev. L. F. Bickford, Pastor.

UNITED PRESBYTERIAN. — Morgan Hall every Sabbath at 11.00 A. M., Sabbath school at 10.00 A. M. Services by Rev. James Kelso, residence Madison Avenue, south of Colorado.

OLIVEWOOD CONGREGATIONAL.— Sunday school and gospel service at Olivewood station. Rev. L. F. Bickford, Pastor. Sunday school at 3.00 P. M. Preaching at 7.00 P. M. every Sunday.

FIRST HOLINESS CHURCH.— Corner Moline Avenue and Illinois Street. Services every Sunday at 10.00 A. M. and 3.00 P. M.

CONGREGATIONAL. — Services at church corner of California Street and Pasadena Avenue every Sunday at 11.00 A. M. and 7.30 P. M.; Sunday school at 9.45. Prayer meeting Wednesday evening at 7.30. Rev. D. D. Hill, Pastor.

FRIENDS' CHURCH.— On corner of Marengo Avenue and Mountain Street. Service Sabbath morning at 11.00. Sunday school 9.45 A. M. Services in the evening at 7.30. Meeting on Wednesdays at 10.00 A. M. Prayer meeting Thursday evening at 7.30.

Business meeting first Saturday in each month. All are cordially invited. R. H. Hartley, Pastor.

UNIVERSALIST CHURCH. — Corner Raymond and Chestnut. Services at 11.00 A. M. Sunday school at 10.00 A. M. Rev. Everett L. Conger, Pastor, residence Howard Place.

GERMAN METHODIST. — At old M. E. Church, corner Ramona Street and Worcester Avenue. Sunday school at 9.15 A. M., and preaching at 10.30 A. M. and 7.30 P. M. Rev. L. E. Schnider, Pastor. Young people's meeting 6.30 P. M. Prayer meeting Wednesday evening 7.30.

SOUTH PASADENA SUNDAY SCHOOL. — Every Sunday afternoon at 3.00, in the South Pasadena Schoolhouse. George W. Wilson, Superintendent. Preaching every second and fourth Sunday in the month at 4.00 P. M.

METHODIST EPISCOPAL. — Corner Colorado Street and Marengo Avenue. Services at 11.00 A. M. Services at 7.30 P. M. by P. F. Bresee, D. D., Pastor. Sunday school at 9.45 A. M.

CALVARY PRESBYTERIAN. — Services in College Building, Columbia and Orange Grove Avenue. Rev. A. M. Merwin, Pastor.

CHRISTIAN.— DeLacey Street, between Colorado and Kansas Streets. Services every Lord's day at 11.00 A. M. and 7.30 P. M. Sunday school at 9.00 A. M. Prayer meeting Wednesday evening at 7.30 P. M. All are invited.

PRESBYTERIAN. — Colorado Street and Worcester Avenue. Rev. M. N. Cornelius, Pastor. Residence Worcester Avenue. Services 11.00 A. M. and 7.00 P. M. Sunday school at 9.45 A. M. Prayer meeting

Wednesday evening at 7.30. Strangers cordially invited. Seats free.

BAPTIST.— Corner of Fair Oaks and Locust. Sabbath services at 11.00 A. M. and 7.30 P. M. Sabbath school at 9.45 A. M. Young people's prayer meeting at 6.45 P. M.; Wednesday evening prayer meeting at 7.30. Thursday evening meeting of young people for Bible study 7.30. Rev. C. E. Harris, Pastor.

GERMAN SERVICES. — Services in the German language held every Sunday at 3.00 P. M. Prayer meeting Friday evening at 7.30 in the Baptist church on Fair Oaks Avenue. All Germans are cordially and kindly invited to attend. F. C. Koehler, Pastor, residence Orange Place.

EPISCOPAL.— All Saints Parish, chapel on Colorado Street. Adult Bible class and Sunday school at 9.45 A. M. Morning service at 11.00 A. M. Holy Communion first Sunday in month 12.15 P. M. Evening service at 7.30. Seats free. Strangers cordially welcomed. Rev. John D. H. Browne, Rector.

CATHOLIC. — Corner Bellefontaine and Pasadena Avenue. Services every Sunday morning at 10.00. Rev. Father Cullen officiates.

STREET RAILWAY GUIDE.

City Railroad, from Colorado Street and Raymond Avenue, north to Chestnut, west to Fair Oaks, thence to North Pasadena Cemetery and Arroyo Park. Cars leave Pasadena for Washington Street and Los Robles Avenue every twenty minutes until 6.00 P. M., then thirty minutes past each hour. Cars leave Pasadena for the cemetery each hour until 5.00 P. M., then cars stop at Dakota Street. Cars leave Pasadena for

Arroyo Park twenty minutes past each hour until
5.20 P. M.

West Pasadena Railroad, from Colorado Street and
Fair Oaks Avenue, west and north to San Rafael
Hills, *via* Arroyo Seco.

Highland Railroad, from Raymond, along Broadway to Colorado, thence east to Lake Avenue, and
north to New York Avenue. Cars run every hour
during the day.

Pasadena Railway, from Orange Grove Avenue and
Columbia Street, east to Fair Oaks Avenue, north to
Chestnut, east to Summit, north to Villa, east to
Marengo Avenue, north to Illinois, east to Moline.
Cars run every half hour from 6.30 A. M. to 8.00 P. M.
First car Sundays at 8.45 A. M.

Colorado Street Railway, from Colorado Street and
Fair Oaks Avenue, east to Hill Avenue, thence south
to San Pasqual Street. Also from corner Colorado
and Fair Oaks, east to Lake Avenue, thence north
on Lake, past Olivewood to Villa Street, thence east
on Villa to Allen Avenue. Also from Colorado and
Fair Oaks, east to Los Robles Avenue, south on Los
Robles to California, thence east on California to
Lake Avenue, north on Lake to San Pasqual, thence
east on San Pasqual to Wilson Avenue. Cars run
every fifteen minutes. Late cars to all entertainments.

SPANISH LOCAL NAMES AND THEIR MEANING.

Pasadena — Crown of the Valley.
Las Flores — The Flowers.
Linda Vista — Beautiful View.
El Retiro — The Retreat.
San Gabriel — St. Gabriel.
El Molino — The Mill.
Los Robles — The Oaks.
El Monte — The Brush.
Los Angeles — The Angels.
San Juan Capistrano — St. John, the Chanter.
San Luis Obispo — St. Louis, the Bishop.
San Luis Rey — St. Louis, the King.
San Marcial — St. Michael.
Albuquerque — Family Name.
Buena Vista — Good View.
Grande Vista — Grand View.
Arroyo Vista — River View.
Belle Vista — Fine View.
Hermosa Vista — Handsome View.
Cajon Pass — Box Pass.
Colorado — Red.
El Paso del Norte — The North Pass.
Coronado — The Crowned.
El Llano Estacado — The Meadows.
Gloreta — Pleasant Valley.
Azusa — Family Name.
Alamitos — Little Poplars.
Duarte — Family Name.
Ensenada — Small Bay.
Escondido — Hidden.
La Canyada — Little Valley.

Elsinore — Home of Hamlet.

Garvanzo — Pea.

Las Casitas — Little Homes.

El Temblores — Earthquake (early name of the San Gabriel River).

Ramona — Spanish Christian Name.

Santa Monica — St. Monica.

La Ballona — The Bayou.

San Diego — St. James.

La Puente — The Bridge.

Monte Vista — Mountain View.

La Jolla — The Caves.

Las Vegas — The Meadows.

Mesa — Table-land.

San Joaquin — St. Joacim.

Santa Jenoveve — St. Genevieve.

Sierra Madre — Mother Mountain.

Tia Juana — Aunt Jennie.

Trinidad — The Trinity.

Val Verde — Green Vale.

Elevado — Elevated.

Las Tablas— The Tables.

Piedra Grande — Big Rock.

San Jacinto — St. Hyacinth.

Sacramento — Sacred Mind.

San Francisco — St. Francis.

Mt. Diablo — Devil's Mountain.

INDEX.

INDEX. 141

www.ingramcontent.com/pod-product-compliance
Lightning Source LLC
Chambersburg PA
CBHW021123020726
47500CB00003B/889